What Shirley Missed

What Shirley Missed

Donna Wootton

Donna Wootton

First Edition

Hidden Brook Press
www.HiddenBrookPress.com
writers@HiddenBrookPress.com

What Shirley Missed
Donna Wootton

Cover Design – Richard M. Grove
Layout and Design – Richard M. Grove

Typeset in Garamond
Printed and bound in Canada
Distributed in USA by Ingram,
        in Canada by Hidden Brook Distribution

Library and Archives Canada Cataloguing in Publication

Title: What Shirley missed / Donna Wootton.
Names: Wootton, Donna, 1947- author.
Description: First edition.
Identifiers: Canadiana (print) 20190107529 | Canadiana (ebook) 20190107545 | ISBN 9781927725757
        (softcover) | ISBN 9781927725764 (EPUB) | ISBN 9781927725771 (Kindle)
Classification: LCC PS8645.O68 W43 2019 | DDC C813/.6—dc23

For Roy

1950-2018

Contents

Chapters

– Shirley's Bucket List – *p. 1*

– Loyal Felicia – *p. 10*

– Tony To The Rescue – *p. 14*

– Out of Jail – *p. 23*

– After Sixty – *p. 31*

– The Bletch – *p. 38*

– The Bridge Club – *p. 43*

– The Prom Parade – *p. 47*

– The Prom Dance – *p. 53*

– At the Clubhouse – *p. 57*

– Father's Day – *p. 61*

– Strumming on the Banjo – *p. 70*

– Dealing the Cards – *p. 76*

– Graduation – *p. 82*

– The Golf Tournament – *p. 86*

– Dellport Farmers' Market – *p. 96*

– At the Beach – *p. 103*

– Maud – *p. 108*

– A Demonstration – *p. 113*

– At The Police Station – *p. 119*

– Community Service – *p. 123*

– People Will Talk – *p. 129*

– Stars Above – *p. 134*

– Telling Lies – *p. 140*

– The Road Trip – *p. 146*

– Gone Fishing – *p. 151*

– A Dark Night – *p. 156*

– A Summer Cold – *p. 162*

– Family First – *p. 169*

– Death – *p. 173*

– Goodbye and Good Luck – *p. 178*

– Crash – *p. 187*

– Mourning – *p. 192*

– Visitation – *p. 199*

– The Funeral – *p. 205*

– Reception – *p. 211*

Book Club Questions and Discussion Points – *p. 214*

What Readers Should NOT
       Miss from What Shirley Missed – *p. 216*

A Short Bio Note – *p. 221*

Chapter 1

Shirley's Bucket List

Shirley Palmer opened her front door.

"How could you?" Pamela barged past her mother. "What were you thinking?" she said as she stomped into the hallway without hugging her mother or even giving Shirley a polite greeting.

"Calm down, sweetie. Tell me what's upset you."

Shirley was sure she knew exactly what was bothering Pamela but she needed time to think through her response. What could she say? Where to begin? How much did Pamela know? Shirley supposed her daughter was feeling distraught and would become hysterical if she found out the whole story.

The two women were unaware they had a witness. Felicia was dusting in the front room. Now she made herself small by disappearing into a corner. Her heart was racing. Although she had witnessed many conflicts between mother and daughter she knew this confrontation was different. Everything about the tone of their dispute was dire. Pamela was standing with her back to Felicia railing at her mother and blocking the passage to the door. If Felicia tried to leave the room she feared Pamela would see her then she would be drawn into their argument. Felicia didn't want to be part of anyone's disputes, least of all theirs.

Pamela stood her ground. "Start from the beginning, Mother. Tell me again why my husband, your son-in-law, is in police custody."

Felicia had known Shirley's daughter since she was a teenager. That was in 1980 when Felicia had arrived to look after the household. She knew that Shirley was, as usual, lacking in true insight. She always underestimated her daughter. Shirley was a carefree soul who never stuck to the facts or spoke truthfully. Yet Felicia didn't think of her employer as a liar. Shirley was simply self-absorbed. Her daughter was a loyal soul who right now felt betrayed by the very person she should be able to trust. This was a common thread in their relationship.

"Stop having kittens," Shirley interrupted. Then she smiled, not with a grin, but with a hopeful smile. It was meant to help Pamela calm down. Shirley looked past Pamela.

Pamela turned and saw the reason for her mother's smile. Her stepfather was coming down the stairs. "What's all this then?"

Some moments are like an epiphany. This moment was just that for Pamela. Here was the saviour, the man who had married her mother when she returned to town with a sweet two-year-old girl in tow; the man who had saved her and her mother from shame and poverty; the man who had given them a comfortable house, a respectable life and a future. Pamela had never known her real father. She only knew that he had abandoned them. Her mother said he was not the man Anthony Palmer was. Shirley wouldn't allow her daughter to track down her real father saying he was a bad man and they were better off without him. According to her mother, Pamela should leave well enough alone since Tony was not a bad man. Tony was a good man. He was only a couple of inches taller than Pamela and Shirley. Nothing intimidating about Tony. He may be the inheritor of a local family business and an established life, but he was no terrorizing patriarch. He was soft and sweet. Pamela loved him. His brown hair had turned grey. His undefined muscles had turned soft. His neck was thick. His v-neck cardigan showed the slouch and girth of his back and stomach. Although he was a familiar figure in Pamela's life it was as if she was seeing him for the first time. She never called him her guardian or stepfather. He was a solid presence in her life, her father, but now Pamela was seeing her stepfather for what he was to her mother. Her saviour.

"Clinton's in jail and it's her fault."

"Now, now. Let's not be too hasty to blame," said Shirley.

Pamela knew as soon as the words were out of her mouth that she had spoken unwisely. Yet her anger was stronger than her perception. She was experiencing a split mind. Her mother was, and always had been, exasperating. Shirley was not a strong maternal figure. She behaved like an older sister. She was a voyeur into Pamela's life, especially since adolescence when Shirley became nosy about Pamela's development. Pamela only came to fully realize this since being married to Clinton who talked to her about what her mother was doing by interfering in their married life. Yet they'd never talked about her mother's married life. What kind of a married life does an immature woman have with a man who is more a father figure than an equal partner?

"No, let's not be too hasty," Pamela said, risking sounding sarcastic; but why not be sarcastic given her new understanding of her parents' marriage? "Tell us what you have been doing today with Clinton? Tell us everything."

"Start from the beginning, Shirley." Then Tony turned to Felicia. "Could you please bring us a pot of tea?"

Startled to learn that Felicia had been in the room all this time, Pamela collapsed onto the couch. It had soft, billowy cushions that rose with her weight and never settled flat but hugged her body like a duvet. The couch faced the large, marble fireplace. Two wing chairs flanked both sides of the fireplace and Shirley chose to take a seat in one while Tony sat beside Pamela on the couch. This seating arrangement pleased Pamela. She felt like she had an ally.

"I drove," Shirley said, recollecting her decision to take her car rather than let Clinton drive. "I told him that no one would remember my car. It's neutral, a Chevy sedan for God's sakes." Surely they all remembered why she drove such a bland vehicle. Shirley was persuasive with Clinton, but remembers she nearly got impatient with him when she argued why she needed to be the driver. Her car was mid-sized, a light grey tone. "So I said to Clinton that no one seeing us come and go would remember my car, but they would notice his red pick-up truck. Anyone at the house peeping through the curtain could describe his car to the law. Besides, it's high off the ground and hard to climb in and out of the seats. Fine for the children, but not for a mother-in-law." Shirley looked at Pamela, hoping she was gaining her sympathy. "I admit I got a bit testy with Clinton because he kept insisting on driving, but I figured he was doing me a huge favour. Clinton was my best bet for buying marijuana."

"What?" Pamela pushed herself to the front of the sofa.

Anthony stood up and faced his wife. "What were you thinking? You wanted to buy drugs?" He started pacing back and forth in front of the sofa.

"I made Clinton promise not to tell anyone, especially Pamela." Shirley looked pleadingly at her daughter. "He told me he hadn't smoked the stuff in years, not since becoming a father, but he thought that nowadays the stuff was stronger so he didn't know how much we'd need for a pan of brownies. He also told me that I could get the recipes and the dope off the internet which just shows you what the world has become."

"No, Clinton didn't say anything to me about your madcap scheme. So you just wanted to make a batch of brownies for your bridge ladies?"

Shirley sank into her seat. Her daughter knew her well. Pamela seemed to resent her time playing bridge with her friends and Tony's sister. Pamela had a good relationship with her aunt. She had a good relationship with Felicia. Pamela knew how to get along with people. Where was Felicia?

"And why aren't you in jail, too?" Anthony asked. "Were you caught trying to buy marijuana?" Tony didn't let his wife go on. "I hope you don't have a criminal record now?"

"Well, you see," Shirley began, "I also insisted we wear plain clothes: we drove a nondescript car, we wore nondescript clothes - all to not draw attention to ourselves."

Her audience of two were attentive. Unbidden came the memory of Clinton studying her veined hands gripping the steering wheel. Just as she had forced her fingers to relax, Shirley forced away any doubts or uncomfortable memories of the morning's events. Then remembering she'd taken off her wedding rings and left them at home in her jewelry box where they were still safely stored, Shirley folded her hands in her lap. She was almost tempted to share how much foresight she'd shown by putting her rings away because she didn't want the kind of crooks who sold illegal merchandise thinking she was a rich, old woman - a pushover. They'd fleece her for more than the stuff was worth on the street. "You see I was wearing my wide brimmed straw hat."

Her husband sat down and he and her daughter looked at her in confusion. Saved again, Felicia entered the room with a tray of tea fixings. Shirley kept her hands folded, thinking how clever she'd been wearing that hat. Not only did it hide her face from the dealers, it also hid her from any road cameras they passed. But what she hadn't planned on was that the police must have had a stakeout right where the guys were selling the drugs. How was she going to explain her getaway?

Shirley let her cup sit untouched. She liked a hot cup of tea but she didn't want to show her hand. She remembered chewing gum. Normally she chastised her son-in-law for his foul habit, especially when he came to the dinner table with a wad of it in his mouth looking for a place to park it when he was ready to chew real food. Yet she felt nervous enough to want to chew gum.

"Clinton didn't believe me when I said I had never smoked a joint. He figured that because I was part of the boomer generation I must have experienced what everyone was experimenting with during the sixties and seventies. But I didn't. I lived through the era of free love. Of course that's how I ended up with Pamela."

"Mother."

"Oh, sweetie. It's alright. I told Clinton in no uncertain terms that you were not the result of free love but of my falling in love with the wrong guy. That mishap resulted in our shot-gun wedding that ended up in a terrible marriage that drove me back to Dellport." Shirley smiled at Tony.

"Alright, Shirley, cut to the chase," Tony said.

Shirley used her right hand to lift the china cup and took a sip of tea to stall for time. Clinton took the opportunity of being in the car alone with Shirley to tell her that he thought

Pamela should look up who her real father was. His impertinence nearly resulted in an outright brawl, but Shirley bit her tongue. She had enough sense to brush off Clinton's suggestion and focus on the task at hand. Not happy with being dismissed, Clinton pointed out that she was exceeding the speed limit.

Shirley immediately put on the brake. Normally she kept to the speed limit. Just then a long line of motorcycles roared past them. Their echoing sound reminded Shirley of something else she needed to try before she was too old. Her bucket list was different from most people's. Others included on their bucket list what she'd already done thanks to the indulgence of Tony. As well as getting high on pot, Shirley wanted to ride a motorcycle. As a young mother she'd missed all the fun.

Shirley could feel Clinton studying her out of the corner of his eye. She could feel her blood pressure rising. He'd told her he no longer smoked dope. He wasn't even interested in supporting those who wanted to legalize it. Most of them were washed out hippies making excuses for medical use. If others wanted to board the bus of those taking up the cause, they had a right to do so, but not him. Don't come knocking on his door. Shirley knew he was rude enough to slam it in their faces. Don't bother giving him a call. Shirley heard how often he had slammed the phone down when the shrill ring of an unsolicited phone call disturbed the peace at home, especially if Pamela was working. Don't ask him to join a demonstration.

Something else Shirley needed to do, join a demonstration, but for now, she judged that while Clinton no longer needed to get high, he still needed to temper his tongue. Whenever Shirley criticized him, Clinton claimed she needn't worry. He wasn't going to reach a ripe old age. That was his self-defense for anything he did that didn't meet with her standards. Why live life in moderation if your body was a ticking time bomb? His own dad had died young. He never saw 60. Probably best. If he'd lived longer he would have become intolerable. Even on good days he was cranky and impatient. Think how bad he would have been if he'd had real aches and pains, some genuine reasons for complaints.

"When I had driven a long way I asked Clinton how much further, and he said we weren't far, maybe less than ten minutes away." Again Shirley had to bite her tongue, swallow her words. Now was not the time to argue that she had asked about distance, not time. Normally she would have taken perverse delight in reminding him what a nincompoop he was. She was stuck with him. He was her partner in crime. If Pamela ever found out, she would tell her mother that she should feel ashamed of herself, roping Clinton into her madcap scheme, traveling on back roads to retrieve a bit of missed experience like some perpetual teenager. How had Shirley managed to coerce Clinton? The sad truth was that he was like a perpetual teenager too. Long-faced, soft-jawed, he let her boss him around, or at least, he appeared to let her. Mostly Clinton did his own thing. After his father died Clinton had become the man-of-the-house. His mother depended on him. So what if he got a little high on soft drugs or drank too much now and then. His mother and his wife excused him. They weren't ones to pick an argument or needlessly needle a person.

Shirley realized she was stalling too long. Her husband and daughter were staring at her from across the room sitting comfortably side by side on the sofa. "You see, Clinton was no sooner in the door at the dealers than I saw a parade of police cars approach. Since I'd kept the car idling I managed to carefully put the gear into reverse."

"Where were you?"

"I'm not too sure, Tony. Clinton knew the way but I backed into the bushes to hide and when half the cops were inside the place and the other half stationed outside the door I quietly put the gear into drive and slowly drove away."

Chapter 2

Loyal Felicia

Felicia left number 11 Grove Avenue feeling shaken, like her bones had come loose from her skin. She tried to focus on her surroundings. Usually she appreciated the canopy of trees and the late afternoon birdsong in this upscale neighbourhood, but today Felicia was oblivious to the wonders of nature. She was in her own head walking like an automaton along the familiar route to the green grocer where she bumped into the corner of a wooden crate that stuck out over the outdoor display shelf like an over-sized trunk. Felicia looked down at the pile of cantaloupes from Mexico that smelled overly ripe which was better than the green ones at the supermarket that had no smell. The heavy scent made her dizzy so she rested her palm on one round melon on top only to have it shift which resulted in some melons toppling onto the sidewalk.

When Felicia had arrived at the Palmer's household she was ostensibly there to look after the toddler, Johnny. He was Shirley's young son. However Felicia grew very close to the daughter, too. Felicia was only two years older than Pamela so she was like the big sister Pamela never had. At that time Shirley didn't like the way Felicia rolled her 'l's' (My child will develop a lisp!) so Felicia nicknamed the teenager 'Pammy' which Pamela never minded because she instantly liked Felicia.

"What's bothering you today, Felicia? Usually you have a big smile on your face." Gus talked and worked in one continuous task. He wasn't just selling produce; he was engaging his loyal customers who mattered to him like family. Gus stooped to pick up the fallen melons.

Felicia knew there was no point faking happiness. Unlike her, also, to gossip, but she couldn't help spill the beans about Clinton being in jail, in police custody over drug charges. She didn't say anything about the battle between Shirley and her daughter. That would be gossiping. Felicia knew better than to reveal too much. She felt uncomfortable talking in public about private lives. Usually it was enough with Gus to simply pass the time of day. Yet why hide what he would soon know in bits and pieces from other customers? Her head was bursting with the news of Shirley and Clinton's transgression. Felicia felt disloyal. She'd been loyal to the family for so long and now she was betraying them.

Too late she offered to help him. He was selling the melons cheap, ripe and bruised, buyer beware. She followed Gus inside his store where the ceiling was low and the light was dim. More display cases held a wide variety of imported fruits and vegetables that were in perfect condition and expensive. Felicia stuffed some mangoes into a plastic bag and took it to the cash register.

Gus tutted and shook his head muttering about the behaviour of the privileged. He knew Felicia's background well enough that he felt she was like-minded when it came to the irresponsible and unlawful habits of the young and not so young. Hadn't they come to this country to better the lives of their children? As far as he was concerned people who let their children lead decadent lives were guilty of neglect. That included the likes of Shirley Palmer. Besides, wasn't Clinton Croft an adult? Didn't he have children of his own? More tutting. More head shaking. "Let me weigh those for you," he offered, extending his hand to Felicia.

"Thanks, Gus."

"I'm closing up shop soon, Felicia."

"You are? I'm sorry to hear that. Are you retiring?"

"Yes," Gus said ringing in the cost of her produce. "Business not so good anymore. I'm not needed here. We're going back to the old country. We can build ourselves something very nice there."

"I'll miss you, Gus, but you and your wife deserve happiness."

"Thanks. You are a lovely lady."

Felicia had fled to Canada from Chile with relatives and family friends after the military murdered her father in the 1973 coup. She was ten years old when they came and she found it difficult to learn English, unlike her little brother, Roberto, who at 3 took to English like a native speaker. Roberto stayed in Vancouver where he flourished. He was educated, a lawyer, skilled as a trilingual speaker of English, Spanish, and French. What would he think? She would call him. He knew about people going to jail. Just the idea of being behind bars terrified Felicia. So did breaking the law. She had never lost her faith in democracy. For 35 years she had blessed her adopted country for offering her a peaceful life. What was Shirley thinking by deliberately breaking the law? That woman had some crazy ideas but never unlawful ones. Felicia agreed with Gus that Shirley Palmer was spoiled. She was like a child. Felicia blamed Tony for that. He spoiled his wife. What good did spoiling people ever do? Better to work hard and not ask for too much. Shirley had no sense of what the rest of the world was like. By the time Felicia reached home with her bags from the green grocer she felt desperate. She felt like a foreigner. For decades she'd made this country home, but in an instant, she could be made to feel like she didn't belong.

Chapter 3

Tony To The Rescue

Anthony Palmer dropped Pamela off at her home having convinced her that her presence was not needed at the jail house; that, in fact, it was better for her to be at home when her children arrived since they may have heard something. "You know how quickly rumours spread around town." Tony had lived his entire life in town and he knew the old timers well. There was a flux of new arrivals and he wasn't as familiar with them as Pamela was. In her line of work as a community care provider she often visited clients in their homes. Since selling the hardware store, Tony had started volunteering with the local Welcome Wagon, a community service that provided new residents with freebies. While in business he'd supported the company as it gave him visibility. Now he felt he could give back because he had profited from the service. Whenever he thought newcomers needed more than what the Welcome Wagon gave them, he would let her know. That way he felt like he was part of the network but hardly intimate with their lives.

While the caution was meant to relax her, it only served to loosen her tongue. Pamela remained seated in his car, still distraught. Finally she said, "Clinton must have taken the day off work. He never told me he was taking the day off. Why would he take the day off work to do something like this? I really don't understand."

"I'm sure there's a simple explanation." Tony looked over at her. Pamela spoke through funneled lips that she now pressed together. Her mouth had gone from full and open to narrow and closed. He did not know how to calm her so he sat and waited for her to finish sharing her thoughts.

"Since spring they've been giving employees long weekends, on a rotating basis." She moved her head in quick short shakes. Clearly she was in no hurry to get out of the car.

"Is that so?" Again Tony looked at Pamela not knowing how best to calm her. She was easily agitated, always had been. He often wondered if it was in her blood, not quite hot blooded, but blood that came from her birth father. She was olive-skinned and dark haired, unlike her mother who had pale skin and light red hair. Also, Pamela was not carefree like her mother. She was a worrier.

Without saying another word Pamela unfastened her seat belt and got out of the car. She was deep in thought. Tony watched her walk up the sidewalk as she held herself erect and stiff. Usually she had a light step, not bouncy like Lily, but not heavy like now. Tony kept his eyes on her until she was safely indoors then he drove to Julie Baxter's house. Julie would be able to help. He had known her since she was a child. They had grown up together, studied together, celebrated family milestones together.

Being a Baxter Julie was from a long line of distinguished members of the community. In fact, her great-great-great grandfather had been the first mayor of Dellport, the small town on the shore of Lake Huron. Still a small town but growing. Still a small town but changing. Julie's mother, Dorothy Baxter, was an old family friend of Tony's mother, Maud Palmer. Dorothy resided with Julie and her husband, Christopher James, in one of the big, old, historic houses close to the main street. They had renovated the 19th century home to give them modern amenities but kept the original features that gave it its charm: floor level mouldings, wooden sash windows, original French pocket doors. Their house was just around the corner from where Anthony grew up. Dorothy had lived with her daughter ever since Mr. Baxter passed away twelve years earlier. Julie insisted it was that or move into the newly renovated retirement home. Formerly it was the regional hospital until the government closed it down to build a larger facility. That's where Maud lived in her dotage. Unlike Maud, Dorothy did not suffer from senility. She was fortunate that way. She greeted him at the front door. "Come in Anthony. Are you here to see Christopher?"

"Julie actually," Tony said stepping across the threshold.

"Well she's not here." Dorothy squinted at him as if she was suspicious of his motive for visiting them at home.

"It's alright, Mother." Christopher came up behind his mother-in-law and extended his hand to greet Tony. "She's on her way."

"Unofficial business, eh?" Now Dorothy had her eyelids raised as if she was catching a whiff of a secret plan.

"Something like that," Tony admitted. He followed Christopher into the study, a paneled room opposite the parlor where Dorothy returned to sit with her book. "She's a sharp one," Tony said quietly. Christopher agreed and made small talk with him until Julie arrived.

After greeting her mother, Julie came into the study. Then she closed the door behind Christopher and sat opposite Tony on a leather chair. "How can I help you, Tony?"

"Sorry about wanting to meet you here instead of at your office but I would like to keep this meeting discreet. I'm hoping I can solve this without turning it into a legal case."

As Tony explained how his son-in-law ended up in custody Julie listened attentively, her eyes on him unblinking. After he finished she turned her head and pondered the situation silently. Then she raised her chin and again looked at him directly. She asked him a few more questions before saying, "This is my personal advice, Tony. Clinton's been clean for a dozen years or more. The cops know the dealers and they know Clinton's not one of them. Go see him. The chief will let you talk to him privately if you ask respectfully. Make a case that he was taken there by an old friend and just happened to be at the wrong place at the wrong time. One of those louses will do him a favour and corroborate. Especially if he thinks it will help him get off lightly."

The new police headquarters was on the edge of town. Tony parked his car in the Visitors lot between two other vehicles to keep it hidden from view. As soon as he stepped out of his car he felt the heat of the day that radiated off the pavement. There was a long cement ramp leading up to the red brick building that Tony chose instead of taking the three levels of stairs. He wiped his brow before he entered the air conditioned building. "I'm here to see Chief Albert Schroeder," he told the receptionist. After she announced, "Anthony Palmer's here to see you," she immediately buzzed the door open for him. The police chief met him in the hallway and led him into his private office. He was a tall man, over six feet, and fit. He walked with a swaying gait.

"This is a terrible business," Tony began and sat in the chair that he was directed to take.

"It's a great day for us, Mr. Palmer. We've been trying to catch these boys at it for months. Sorry about Clinton, though. I don't know how he got caught up in the mess." He sat behind his desk where he seemed a normal height, his tallness coming mostly from his long legs.

"Well, that's why I'm here. Could I talk to him? Find out what happened?"

"If you think it will help." He cupped his fingers and held them under his chin.

Tony felt he should go softly. "Well, it might. I'm sure you don't want to have to lay any more charges than necessary and I don't want to have to start legal proceedings. Sorry, that's not a threat, but you can imagine how worried the family is."

After nodding the chief dropped his hands to lay them on his desk and said, "Of course. Wait here and I'll bring Clinton to you."

While waiting Tony surveyed the chief's office. He saw the familiar family photographs on display. The largest one pictured what looked like a big extended family. A smaller one pictured Albert Schroeder with his wife at a celebratory event. Between the two windows hung many degrees and diplomas, just like Ramsey had displayed on his walls. Tony was familiar with the old station house as he knew the departed chief, Ramsey Reisch, well. Albert Schroeder had arrived at a time when budgets were frugal, especially after building costs for this new place escalated. There were some who wanted to replace the local force with the county police or even a bigger division. The only concession made to those lobbyists was to hire someone outside the township to replace Ramsey Reisch. Schroeder came with a good reputation for keeping those in uniform accountable to high professional standards. Yet he was human. Tony could now vouch for that. He had experience in how the police operated.

His son, Johnny, was always getting into trouble. He'd needed a bit of guidance and Ramsey knew what to do to redirect the local youth. Julie Baxter had often served as his lawyer when needed on his visits to the police station no matter what balls-up Johnny found himself in. Tony no longer knew where his son was living but he suspected that Pamela did. She'd always taken care of her little brother, better than Shirley did. Tony hated to admit that but it was the truth. Shirley always made excuses for their son. Tony tried to reform him and he deserved full marks for trying but, in the end, he had failed Johnny. Sometimes raising a child could end up a total debacle.

When Chief Albert Schroeder returned he left Clinton with Tony in his office to talk privately. As soon as Clinton started into how he wasn't going to betray Shirley, Tony silenced him and started asking questions. Did he know any of the dealers personally? Was he an old friend from former days? Could he be a witness to the fact that Clinton was not one of their gang? Would he corroborate a story that Clinton was just visiting him? "It's worth a try," Clinton said.

Tony went to get Chief Albert Schroeder and asked him if they could interview Doug Nicholl in his office. When Doug was brought into the office Chief Albert Schroeder stayed. Anthony introduced himself as Clinton's father-in-law. "He tells me that you're an old school chum?"

"Yeah. That's right. We go way back. But, hey, I haven't seen this dude in more than a dozen years." He grinned showing a mouthful of narrow teeth.

Tony examined Doug intensively. He was as skinny as an adolescent. "Yes, so you were happy to have him visit today for old times sake?" Tony nodded his head in confirmation. Would this wasted druggie catch the message?

Doug smiled broadly. "I sure was. Bad timing though, eh,

Clinton? You couldn't ha' picked a worse time. We thought maybe you brought the cops. Some of my friends think you're the informer. I think we should set them straight, eh, Chief? We don't want Clinton here taking the rap for something he didn't do."

"Well Doug, if you could help me out with that I'd be much obliged."

Doug was shaking his head now. "I sure can. I can sure be of help. I don't want to get my old buddy here in trouble. There's enough trouble behind bars already."

"You wait here, Doug, while I escort these gentlemen out."

Doug was grinning from ear to ear. "Nice seeing you, Clinton. We'll see you again soon."

"Sure thing," Clinton said. As he left the office with Tony and Chief Albert Schroeder he mumbled he wouldn't go anywhere near Dougie again. "Not in this lifetime."

The police chief directed his secretary to write up a discharge for Clinton Croft. While waiting for the typist he passed the time of day with Tony by asking him about the golf club.

"Do you play?" Tony asked. He kept one eye on the secretary to reassure himself that this was really happening. There was a buzz of quiet noise in the air from powered computers and working printers. As well as secretaries, uniformed personnel moved around the open space talking quietly. Some sat at work stations.

"Yes, I do, but not here in town. You know I don't live here. I commute each day. It's better. My wife didn't want to pull up roots when I got the promotion."

"Can't blame her," Tony said. "If you'd like to play at the course here I can certainly take you as a guest sometime."

"I'd like that," Chief Albert Schroeder said. "Give me an opportunity to get to know the local community better." He took the discharge sheet from his secretary and read over the paper. "Now if you'll just sign here and mark the date, you're free to go, Mr. Croft."

Tony looked over Clinton's shoulder and scanned the document that Clinton signed and dated, Friday, June 13, 2008. Then he chuckled out loud. "Friday, the thirteenth."

Outside Tony tried to keep an excitable and noisy Clinton calm. "Don't start yelling and cheering. They'll hear you inside."

"I can't believe how easy that was." In the car Clinton talked on and on about how Shirley had gotten him in trouble. "Thank you, Tony, for getting me off without even a record."

"Let's hope there's no record. If I know the men in uniform they keep a record of discharges as well as convictions." Tony bit his tongue about Shirley. He often kept quiet about his wife. He'd learned in his early years of marriage that she wasn't a reliable woman but assumed from the way other men talked that their wives were the same.

"What do you mean?" Clinton asked.

"Just that. The men in uniform are record keepers and you can bet your boots Albert Schroeder is very good at that and combing the records as we speak."

"On me?"

"On you. On the family. On everyone in custody. If they don't have them uploaded to their computer files they'll be sifting through paper. They'll be in full detective mode having a heyday. It's not often they get to actually convict someone of a real crime."

"That thorough?"

"You don't get to be chief without being thorough. Before

the end of the day he'll know everything about us including how Johnny smashed Shirley's car not so many years ago."

"She did go on about using her car since it's so plain. I have to give her credit. She really thought it through."

"Owning a flashy car only lasted a day."

"Yeah. Never give the keys of your new car to your son. I'll remember that."

"To your children, period."

Chapter 4

Out of Jail

Lily was watching for her father at the front window. Their house was an old, two storey, stucco cottage similar to others on the block. Originally built on large lots these houses were interspersed with more contemporary dwellings built decades earlier when the owners of the cottages severed their lots. Lily's mother liked the charm of the older homes and had kept the casement windows despite the impracticality of them for keeping out the cold or letting the heat escape.

Lily waved when she saw her father arrive and dashed to the door. Clinton waved back to her disappearing figure. He ran up the front stairs with a head full of bright colour: the flash of his daughter against the billowing curtains, the rays of late afternoon sun striking the forsythia bush, the gleam of white on the freshly painted pillars – his work. When Lily burst out the door laughing he grabbed her in his arms and swung her around on the front porch. "Glad you're home, Dad," Lily said as she landed back on her feet.

Pamela followed behind them. "I think your daughter is getting too old to be slung around like that. Remember, she's graduating this month, or had you forgotten that when you left this morning? Which reminds me, young lady, tomorrow we're going shopping for your prom dress."

Slowly Clinton turned to his wife. "You know I wasn't involved in anything."

Pamela hesitated for a moment. "I'm just glad Tony was there to help."

"Me, too." Then Clinton put his arms around both their waists and, with each on either side of him, pulled them indoors and over to the front window. "You must buy a pretty dress for our pretty daughter. Maybe one the same as colour as these sheer curtains." He stretched a swath of material and held it beside his daughter's face declaring how flattering the champagne shade was against her beautiful skin. "There's a pink undertone to it just like your complexion."

Lily blushed. "Dad."

Pamela appraised the two. "I didn't know you could be so flattering."

Tim entered the room and sobered them up with his question. "Were you caught up in a police raid? Do you know that gang?"

Clinton shrugged. "Yes, 'fraid so, but, thanks to your grandpa, I was discharged."

Lily swooned. "Grandpa's the best gentleman ever."

"That's so cool," Tim said. "Tell us more." Clinton and Pamela looked at each other and laughed at their son for saying 'cool'. Then Clinton asked his wife, "Do you remember Dougie Nicholl?"

"I don't."

"You see, that's because your mother is older than me."

"Only by two years."

"In high school two years is eons. You don't remember

Dougie but I'll bet he remembers you. That's how it works. In high school we all looked up to the older kids because we wanted to be like them. Mostly older, but also more accomplished and experienced. Right?"

"Definitely," Tim said. "My friends know my sister but Lily ignores us."

Lily made a face, pulling down the corners of her lips, wrinkling her nose and puffing out her cheeks to show her disgust.

Ignoring his children's behaviour, Clinton continued, "So your mother doesn't remember Dougie Nicholl who was a pot head in high school and still is. You see, today I'm visiting this dude," Clinton swayed from one leg to the other and hurried through his thoughts in case he was asked the obvious question, "when the police raid the joint for drugs which they find in abundance and they put me in the slammer with the gang."

"What's it like?"

"What's what like?"

"Jail. What's it like in jail?" Tim asked.

"Hey, you don't ever want to go there."

"Like Uncle Johnny did," Lily said.

"Dinner's ready," Pamela said. "Come and eat." She ushered her children out of the room ignoring her daughter's comment about her uncle. Sometimes the family contract to forget was as important as any promises to remember. Pamela was bent on having her children remember her half brother for the good in him. That's what she did, always dwelt on the good. It helped with her family and with her line of work. Her determined efforts kept her focused on accomplishing what needed to be done. She hated it when her mother interfered in these efforts which she often unwittingly did just by behaving in her normal fashion. Pamela didn't blame Johnny for flying the coop. He needed to get on with his life too.

Around the table the discussion continued with Clinton holding forth as if he was some returning hero. Tim listened attentively to extract juicy details. Clinton obliged by embellishing his story with descriptive details. "Have you ever been down one of those rough back roads that lead into the rugged hinterland?"

Tim looked blankly at his dad.

"I don't think so. This isn't a place where we go for a Sunday drive. No, this is an area so remote no one who doesn't know their way would dare to go. There was a wooden bridge that was in ruins. It forded a fast running stream. Later a creek that had a muddy bottom had no bridge for cars. The twisted tree trunks cast dark shadows over the car and branches hung so low they scraped the roof of the car. Then the car travelled the narrow tracks to higher ground where the bedrock became the road and there were no signs to point the way so you don't even know if you're going in the right direction." Tim's eyes grew wider as the details piled up to create a scene of a blighted and fractured landscape.

Lily hung on to her father's every word. She seemed wistful, which Pamela attributed to her age. She was a romantic. When her father described how their grandpa asked for a meeting with the drug dealer in the chief of police's office, Lily grew positively awestruck. This admiration for the only grandfather she'd ever known worried Pamela. Tony doted on her, which was what most grandparents naturally did, but Pamela felt conflicted about her mother's past. It wasn't a secret to people in Dellport, but young people had their own interests and that hardly included small town gossip. They were more interested in their own dramas as there was always plenty to share and exploit among the circles of friends who changed their loyalties on a dime. Yet Pamela could not remember sitting down with her children to talk to them, to actually say she had a different father than her younger brother. Did they know? They must. Of course they did, but how did they know? Pamela had amnesia about this and could not decide whether or not to say something to the children at this sensitive time. Why blurt it out? Why remind everyone? They adored their uncle as much as they adored their grandpa. Both Lily and Tim excused Uncle Johnny all manner of misdemeanors. Pamela was not raised to think in terms of Johnny being a half-brother. Now she realized that if she did give it a voice she would reveal to her children that she had an opinion. Their grandpa was not a blood relative. Did it matter? In her heart Pamela knew it didn't. She could trust her children to accept him no matter what his lineage.

Lily and Tim belonged to a younger generation who were more accepting than older people. The real problem was that they had been told a lie, if not directly, then implicitly. The real problem was that Pamela had never disclosed who her birth father was and whose fault was that? Her mother's. It all went back to her and now Pamela was sitting around the table having a conversation with her children that was basically false. The premise was wrong. Clinton, her husband, their father, had not gone to visit Dougie Nicholl. Shirley had driven him there so she could get marijuana so she could make a batch of brownies so she could get high. How exciting a revelation would that be? They'd be clamouring for more. Only the insiders knew. Pamela had two minds functioning as if she was a schizophrenic. Her engaged mind was at the table but her detached mind was churning over all kinds of possibilities.

Everyone helped with the cleaning up, making it an exceptional evening without any arguments about whose turn it was to do kitchen chores. Pamela took some consolation in that family bond. Clinton saw her smiling and, putting down the pot in his hand, came over and gave her a hug. He whispered in her ear and she withdrew saying, "Later."

Raising her hands above her head Lily spun around the kitchen and sang a made-up ditty about only having one more exam before she was finished with high school for good. After that came the night of the prom.

"Who's your date?" Tim asked.

Lily stopped and stood still seemingly not dizzy from her performance. "Rupert."

"Him? He's your boyfriend? Rupert Leach? Are you crazy?"

"He's not my boyfriend. He's just a date for the prom. We're going as friends. We've been in the same grade together forever."

"That's because you don't have a boyfriend. And he doesn't have a girlfriend. You're both nerds."

"You can talk."

"Enough, you two," Clinton said. "We're all very proud of Lily. She's a very accomplished young woman."

Tim gagged.

"Hey, buster. Remember, come September, you'll be on your own with us. No big sister. Be nice now."

"Sure," Tim said twirling the tea towel dangerously close to his sister.

"Come off it."

"That's enough, Tim," Pamela said. "You can go now. Thanks for your help"

"You're welcome," Tim said charging out of the kitchen.

The sound of his pounding up the stairs echoed through the room.

Later, in their bedroom, Pamela confided in Clinton that she knew how he got caught up in the sting. "Who else knows?" he asked.

"Felicia. She was in the room when I went to the house. She wasn't there for the full story but she was obviously troubled by what she did hear."

"Felicia won't say anything."

"No she won't." Then Pamela shared with her husband all her concerns. Everything. A whole litany of woes. Clinton said he had expressed his opinion to Shirley that Pamela should be allowed to trace her real father but Shirley ignored him as usual.

"She'd never allow it, but why do I need her help or consent?"

"You don't. Maybe it's time you did what you want instead of what she wants."

"Clinton, I can't understand how my mother talked you into going today."

"I know. I'm a fool. You know she needled me until I couldn't say no."

Pamela sighed.

"I'm really sorry for what happened," said Clinton.

"Apology accepted. Let's try to put it all behind us. Tomorrow I'm looking forward to going shopping for a dress for Lily. It's all so last minute because she didn't have a date until yesterday. Tim's right. She doesn't have a boyfriend. When she was studying with Rupert and learned that he didn't have a date either, they decided to go together. I'm so happy for her. It's important to be part of that rite of passage. Besides, she really likes dancing."

"I wonder if Rupert does?"

"It doesn't matter. They dance together in a mob. I'm glad I don't have to chaperon."

"Do the teachers?"

"Yes, it's a dry event. No alcohol. The parents' association organized it that way after what happened last year."

"After the accident. Wise choice."

"Let's hope everyone stays safe this year and has a good time." Clinton held her close in bed and she lay in the dark thinking about the difficulties of family.

Chapter 5

After Sixty

The house went dead quiet when Tony left with Pamela. Shirley sneaked upstairs like a thief in her own house and retrieved her diamond rings from the jewelry box on top of the dresser. She pushed them on the ring finger of her left hand and stretched it to admire the glitter. Recently she'd had the rings cleaned and resized. They looked brand new. Her fingers were wrinkled and her hand full of liver spots but the hard crystals showed no wear or tear. Why did her hands show wear and tear when she hardly ever used them except to deal the cards? It wasn't like she had to do heavy housework or stick them into soapy water. None of that seemed to matter to the aging of her hands. Marks of aging seemed indiscriminate. She shook her head and rose. Such reflection was more than she was accustomed to experiencing.

Shirley walked into the en suite bathroom where she stopped in front of the mirror. Her hair was going grey. She'd asked her hairdresser about colouring it but she hadn't yet made up her mind. Her hairdresser said she could not guarantee that a colour rinse would restore Shirley's hair to its original colour since it was a unique shade of red, very pale but robust. Maybe she should let it grow long? Leaning over the sink Shirley looked closely at her roots. Would she get a rinse at her next appointment? If she had her hair cut without getting it coloured she would be left mostly grey. But what if she got it coloured and she ended up a fiery red-head? What would be more embarrassing, being a sixty year old with grey hair or one with long hair? Secretly she wished she could comb the colour upwards, like an act of time travel, going back to when she had beautiful hair. The colour of her hair was her best asset and now she was losing it. Growing old was not fair. Like her hands, her hair showed telltale signs.

Felicia must have left while she was upstairs because the woman was nowhere to be found. She'd left the clean cups stacked with the china tea pot on the tray on the dining room table. Shirley thought it strange that Felicia had not put them away as she was usually very tidy about finishing her jobs before leaving. Nowadays Felicia only came every other day: on Mondays, Wednesdays and Fridays - a suitable arrangement for them. At the start of her employment with the family, Felicia had helped Shirley take care of Johnny who was uncontrollable. He never stopped moving which exhausted Shirley. Once he started school, Shirley kept Felicia in her employment cleaning the house and making the meals. Shirley always did the shopping.

In the kitchen Shirley opened the fridge door. Sure enough Felicia had made her signature meat pies, or hallacas, as she called them. They were made with raisins, green olives and chopped hard-boiled eggs, as well as ground meat. There were enough to feed her and Tony for two nights. On Sunday they were invited to Pamela's for supper and Shirley didn't even speculate on whether or not they were still welcome. She decided to go to the supermarket to get a prepared salad to go with the meat pies.

When Tony came home she told her husband what had happened at the supermarket. She'd bumped into Tony's sister, Jane, who knew all about Clinton being in jail. Tony explained that he'd been discharged which meant he didn't have a criminal record. "I'll call her. Best to set her straight."

"And there's something wrong with the fridge. It keeps making a strange noise."

"What kind of a noise?"

"I don't know," Shirley said. "A buzzing sound."

"Is the fridge working?"

"Oh yes, it's working fine."

"Then it can wait. Let me know when you hear it again so I can listen. Maybe it's something Clinton can fix."

It was just like her husband to ask her for a description of something as ordinary as a noise and it was also just like him to tell Clinton who could fix anything which is why he worked at public works supervising every job in town. As Shirley unwrapped the greens she kept one ear to her husband's side of the conversation. He was emphasizing with his sister that a discharge meant Clinton was freed with no criminal record. Then Shirley heard the name 'Doug Nicholl' as purportedly someone Clinton was meeting when he got caught up in the police raid. Shirley chuckled quietly so as not to reveal that she had overheard the incriminating name. Already she was looking forward to the next bridge club meeting. She knew Jane would have lots to say about the Nicholl family. The father was a character who thought he was better than everyone else because he'd been sent away to a boys' private school. He ended up back in Dellport selling insurance. Now Jane Palmer had the real goods the rumours would fly. The culprit was Doug Nicholl. Shirley could hear the gossips now tut tutting about Hank

Nicholl and his son. She put the meat pies in the toaster oven. They were shaped like turnovers with the pastry edges pinched. They heated better in the toaster oven than in the microwave which made them soggy.

Tony returned and rubbed his palms together. "Something smells good. I hope dinner's ready soon." Nothing more was said about Clinton or jail or marijuana.

On Sunday Tony repeated the same gesture. "That smells like home cooking. Is it one of Pamela's roasts?" he asked while rubbing his palms together.

"I must give credit where credit is due. The whole family pitched in to help," Pamela said.

"We were going to make it simple and have a barbecue but decided, given the downpour, to squelch that idea."

"Don't blame you," Tony said. "That's why we put in the gas line outside and installed the roll out umbrella off the roof. Makes going outside to barbecue much easier. You'll have to come over for Father's Day and let me do the honours."

"Sure thing," Clinton said grinning at his wife. Pamela had wondered if her parents would come so she had phoned earlier. She told her husband that Tony had behaved as if nothing had happened. She wondered if he could have already forgiven him, but Clinton made it very clear that it was Shirley Tony was protecting, not him.

"And you can have a look at our fridge," Tony said. "It keeps making a buzzing sound."

"From the freezer?" Clinton asked. "You have a bottom freezer in that new fridge, right?"

"Yes," Tony said.

"There's a problem with a line at the back. Mate at work had the same problem."

"You don't say. I knew I could count on you. You're a craftsman who can fashion a repair on anything."

"Well it's a bit of a jerry rigged job we did but it works."

Lily, who was standing patiently between her father and grandfather, grabbed her grandmother's hand and dragged her upstairs. "I want to show you my prom dress."

Shirley sat on the edge of her granddaughter's bed and watched Lily pull out an organza dress with a full skirt. "What a wonderful colour," she said smiling with the corners of her lips and tilting her head to the right.

Lily held the dress against the front of her body and smoothed down the skirt. "Thanks, Grandma. Do you like it?"

"It's perfect for you. When's the prom?"

"In a week. On Friday, June 20. I can't wait."

"You're a lucky girl," Shirley said with a wistful sigh recalling how she had missed the high school graduation prom. Before the end of her final year she had already left for the north to work at her uncle's lodge where her world fell apart before the summer was over. "What shoes are you wearing?"

"Oh, I don't know," Lily said looking behind her as if her closet might magically produce a pair.

"Well you have to have shoes and a little purse to match that beautiful dress."

"I haven't thought about accessories."

"Let me buy those for you," Shirley said. "It would make me so happy and proud to be of help. And a shawl. You must have a summer wrap to go around your shoulders."

"Do you think so?"

"Indeed I do." Shirley thought that it was just like her daughter, Pamela, to get the main part right but not all the other parts. Sometimes her mind seemed incomplete, as if she was on another planet. "Where did you buy your dress?"

"At Adele's."

"Good choice," Shirley said about the long-standing ladies clothing store on the main street. "I have an account there. Go back and pick out the matching items. They'll know how to put you together. You'll be the queen of the prom, Lily." Shirley let her pride in her granddaughter glow through every pore of her skin. She knew better than to live vicariously through the younger generation but she also knew she wanted to relish what her own mother missed. She died before Pamela finished high school, not from old age, but from what Shirley could only describe as exhaustion. Hazel seemed tired of life. She'd outlived her husband and buried a son – too much sorrow that tired her out.

"I hardly think so. They don't crown a prom queen anymore, Grandma."

"They don't?"

"No, Mom told me Auntie Jane was crowned prom queen."

"Um," Shirley said rising. "Let's go downstairs."

As soon as Shirley came downstairs Pamela accosted her. "What's this about Felicia leaving?"

"Dear me, Pamela, Felicia isn't leaving. She just took a few days off to go to see her brother."

"In Vancouver?"

"Yes, that's where he lives."

"Why so sudden?"

"Well I don't know. She didn't talk to me. She hardly needs my permission. I'm not worried. She left me with plenty to eat. There's a ton of containers of chicken stew in the freezer."

"Her chicken stew? Cazuela?"

"Yes. You remember it. Tony loves it."

"We all do. It's made with corn and pumpkin."

"And potatoes and green beans. Yes, I know," Shirley said with a hint of impatience. Was her daughter concerned about her mother? Was she asking how she would manage all week without help? Shirley was scheduled to host the bridge club next week. Earlier she thought she would serve hash brownies and give them all a good giggle. She wouldn't be doing that now. She wouldn't even mention it. No point. "Felicia was considerate enough to leave out the teapot and china cups for me to serve the bridge ladies on Thursday."

Pamela choked. "Surely you can take a few cups out of the cabinet."

"Well, of course I can. I'm just saying."

Pamela turned and crashed into her daughter at the bottom of the stairs. "Grandma says we can go back to the store and buy accessories to match my dress."

"Did she now?" Pamela asked her daughter while staring at her mother who could take over when she had a mind to spend money without asking permission.

With stunned gazes Lily and Shirley followed Pamela as she retreated to the kitchen. "Don't worry, dear. Your mother's just a little fraught."

Chapter 6

The Bletch

Paolo Costa, Felicia's husband, was a member of the banjo group that met at a pub called The Bletch every Wednesday night. The Bletcher House was the former customs house so it had historic significance although you'd be hard-pressed from the street to recognize the building as anything but slightly run-down. It offered a place to relax with people from town. Normally Paolo looked forward to the weekly get-together, but as soon as he entered the back room he was accosted. "So we hear your wife has left town."

"No, not left. She went to Vancouver to visit our son and her brother." He thought he should be careful what he said. Their son and his brother-in-law had given them legal advice but Clinton's story had already reached them through the grapevine.

"Defying the law was no laughing matter. Being in jail is serious business," one member said encouraging Paolo to say more.

"Trouble is something to avoid at all costs," said another.

Felicia had been so upset about the whole affair she didn't want to return to the Palmer's house. Over the years she had watched their Johnny get into trouble. She'd always felt protective of him, too, as she identified as his second mother. Yet no one ever sought her advice on raising him.

Paolo simply said, "I agreed that she needed a break from the Palmer household."

"Why didn't you go too?"

He didn't say that he had encouraged her to use their holiday savings to get away. "I'm fine on my own. Our son, Patrick, attends university there and lives with his uncle."

Last Friday when she'd arrived home distraught Paolo had said to her, "Shirley talks too much and thinks too little. Always did." For once Felicia had agreed with him. Usually she was very protective. Paolo saw his opportunity and also said that Shirley was a shirker, which Felicia didn't understand, so he had explained that her employer didn't like work, never had to work, always avoided work. This upset Felicia because she realized that she only had a job because Shirley was a shirker.

Then feeling daring Paolo had said, "Look how her son turned out."

That had the effect of making Felicia weep muttering about their son who was already on a career path and blubbering how she loved Johnny but no one knew where he was and recalling many fond memories like gripping his strong little hand in her palm when they went out together to the playground. After that they had decided that Felicia was not up to returning to work.

At the Bletch no one knew the real story. Paolo understood that immediately. Mostly they were bad mouthing Doug Nicholl and others. They wanted to know if Paolo knew how Clinton Croft got off. Some of the members of the banjo group had opinions on the new chief of police. Paolo thought how Patrick would tell his father not to be scared. They lived in a democracy. They had rights like free speech. People could talk openly about the police. So Paolo listened and kept his mouth shut but he felt uncomfortable listening to their abuse. None of them needed to know what he knew. The night before, he had talked to Patrick who was studying law. Over the telephone he'd reassured his parents about the situation. Paolo and Felicia had him on speaker phone. They could have a three-way conversation in the privacy of their own home. Paolo recognized that as a freedom which he greatly appreciated. They talked for over an hour. Their son advised them to stay mute about what they did know. Sometimes free speech only went so far. They didn't want the whole town questioning them.

Paolo started strumming. It didn't matter that there was no truth to the rumours. When Paolo had talked to his wife and son on Sunday, this time in a three-way conversation with Felicia and Patrick in Vancouver, Paolo had shared with them what people he'd met on the street were saying. He had met people he knew in public places like stores. He told his wife and son what people whispered to him. Patrick had explained that gossip did not fuel the outcome of the law. His father did not need to set the record straight. That was not his responsibility. At the time Paolo had thought it was a strange freedom to have but he knew to take his son's advice. He was lonely with Felicia gone and with no one to talk to about his worries.

After an unusually long delay the group joined him and soon everyone was strumming and singing. Paolo relaxed and forced himself to smile while playing. If anyone were to look closely they would see that his eyes were dull and steady.

At the end of the jam session, Paolo turned his back on the group in an attempt to avoid more talk but one member didn't let him off the hook. While packing up to leave Brenda Bain asked him if he would like a ride home. She was new to town, a lawyer. Last week he'd spoken to her about her studies in law after confiding that his son Patrick was studying to become a lawyer. She understood right away that Patrick had headed to British Columbia to work during the summer months with his uncle because that was where he wanted to live and practice law.

"We support his decision," Paolo had said. Then he'd elaborated to her about the virtues of living on the west coast where the climate was moderate. He'd confided how depressing they had found the winters when they had first moved east. In the dead of winter they often regretted living like shut-ins as they had no skills to pursue outdoor entertainments, yet they also had no desire to learn. When spring came they returned to their habit of taking long evening walks along the beach.

Now he said to Brenda, "It seems unfair that Felicia has had to leave just when she is beginning to enjoy the season."

"And very sad."

Paolo felt Brenda understood. "My wife said we should retire out west. There's no reason to stay. We have no immediate family living in the east."

In the car Brenda asked, "What originally brought you east?"

Paolo told her about being born in Mexico. "When I migrated north I started working in the fields picking crops." Brenda was not smug like others he knew. She seemed like one of those rare people who knew when to retreat. It was not censure but a mild sense of restraint. He guessed she knew what he meant by 'migrating'.

Brenda confided in him. "I have been retained to represent Doug Nicholl. I appreciate your discretion in not talking publicly about the details of the case."

"Yes, my son's advice."

"Well, I've only been showing up on Wednesdays since the spring, and I want to continue, I like the jam sessions, but I'm quickly learning that sometimes it's hard in a small town to become part of a community group. At first I thought the diversion would relax me. I don't want to play darts on Tuesdays or come on Thursdays for trivia night. Maybe I'll be forced to keep my own company and go for walks to relax."

"Only they get you on the street too."

Brenda sniggered like a schoolgirl.

"Sorry," Paolo said as the car came to a stop in front of his house.

"No need to apologize. You caught me off guard there. Behaving professionally has its challenges."

Paolo said, "I think that's the reason why Patrick went west. As much as he wants to be close to us, he has a better chance of becoming a professional under the tutelage of his Uncle Roberto." Smiling broadly Paolo picked up his banjo case and thanked Brenda profusely for giving him a lift. Opening the passenger door he said he hoped that he would see her next week. He needed a comrade in arms who wanted to relax with others, who wanted to play an easy string instrument, who wanted to leave the world outside the door of the pub.

Chapter 7

The Bridge Club

At the front door Shirley greeted her guests. Barbara, who was the last surviving Bletcher, lived with Jane Palmer in her family home. They arrived together and asked after Felicia as they had heard she was gone. Shirley brushed off their concerns and told them that she had had an easy time getting ready for bridge club. She'd only had to get one more cup and saucer out of the cabinet to add to the three Felicia had left out on the dining room table with the teapot and who couldn't make tea. What's more, Shirley had patronized that new little bakery, Sugar something, located on the side street off the main street, across from The Bletch. "Do you know it?"

"No," Barbara said rather abruptly. She hated being reminded that her ancestor's historical establishment was reduced to 'The Bletch'.

"We shouldn't be eating so much sugar," Jane said. She bent her head forward to emphasize her statement. She'd learned to make this move when she was a child growing up with a big brother who could win an argument without any effort. Her head was shaped like Tony's, but her features were dissimilar. He had small brown eyes. Hers were large and brown flecked. He had a high forehead whereas hers was narrow. For that reason she never wore bangs. Her hair was still brown to the envy of the others gathered around the bridge table.

"Is this the latest food fad?" Barbara quizzed. "It's all a myth, you know?" She raised her chin in challenge. She was a religious woman not given in to myths or fads.

The doorbell rang and Shirley opened it to Linda Leach, the fourth for bridge. Somehow they all regained their decorum and asked after one another. Shirley said she was just 'hunky dory' even though she was on her own to prepare everything. Barbara said that Jane was no longer eating sugar to which Jane explained that she had not cut sugar out of her diet completely, just cut back. "So if I have a sweet from the bakery this afternoon then I won't have any dessert after dinner tonight."

"Good for your waistline as well as your blood sugar level," Linda said. She was a soft woman, her voice, her complexion, even the colours she chose to wear were soft.

Jane pulled her brows into a scowl. She never understood that Linda was only trying to be helpful. Instead Jane always thought Linda was criticizing her.

Shirley waved her guests out of the front foyer and led them to the bridge table that she had set up in the living room. They played a round before Jane said that the new young lawyer in town was defending Doug Nicholl which started a long conversation on the criminal activities and the notorious behaviour of the town's worst characters. It was all Shirley could do not to spill the beans. If only she could tell these ladies that she had planned to serve them hash brownies so they could all get high and enjoy an experience that had eluded each of them in their youth. Yet, if she did mention her botched plans, she would reveal the truth. The truth would not go over well. The women would be all over her for more information about who did what and when. Keeping a secret was more than Shirley could stand. She was about to start bragging when Linda changed the topic of conversation to the upcoming prom. This served to further irritate Shirley because Jane reminded them that she had been crowned the prom queen. As if reading Shirley's mind, Jane asked, "But you never got to go to the prom, did you, Shirley?"

Mean Jane, Shirley thought.

Linda said, "I'll be driving my grandson to the prom in my late husband's antique car, a classy Oldsmobile convertible. You might remember it? But I'm scheduled to have cataract surgery in July and I have to admit I don't know if I should get behind the wheel, especially in a car as valuable as the convertible."

"Is that why you've been walking everywhere?" Barbara asked. "You should have told us. We can drive you. Just ask. We'll take you where you want to go."

While Barbara spoke Shirley schemed. "Rupert is taking Lily as his date."

"Is he?" Jane asked. "I'm so glad for them. Won't they make a handsome couple."

"It's just a date for the prom," Linda said. She lowered her chin and raised her eyebrows, an action that was as bold as she ever got.

Shirley piped up, "I'll drive."

Linda beamed. "Thank you, Shirley. That's a wonderful idea. We can sit in the front, proud grandmothers."

"And you'll finally get to go to the prom," Jane said, turning to look directly at her sister-in-law.

"Oh, we won't be going," Linda said. "We're just the drivers."

"Which means you do get to be in the parade," Jane said. "We didn't do anything like that in our day, did we Barbara?"

"No, but we did get dressed up fancy and afterwards we had a party."

"Yes, at the house where we all got drunk."

"We did and I have the pictures to prove it. It was a big deal back then."

"Getting drunk?" Shirley asked.

"No, having a party. It was our first really big party like the adults always had.

"This year it's a dry prom," Linda said.

Shirley stayed mute. Her head was full of images of prom night. She was going and she would dress up and she would dance the night away despite what Linda had to say.

Chapter 8

The Prom Parade

The Oldsmobile was a 1959 convertible coupe. It was long and red with white tail fins. The chrome trim shone. The tires were rimmed in red and white. Shirley touched the gleaming hood and swooned. In a reverie she said to Linda, "I can still picture you and Clarence driving around town with the top down."

"That was decades ago."

"It was. How time flies, especially when you're having fun."

Linda said, "I had it restored and cleaned just for this special night. It's been sitting in the garage for three years, ever since Clarence died. Dellport Auto Shop did a great job though it cost me thousands of dollars."

"How many thousands?" Shirley asked admiring the gleam of the chrome.

Linda refused to reveal to Shirley how many thousands, saying only, "Our grandchildren are worth the expense."

"They are."

"I like your large sunglasses, Shirley. I guess that's what I'll have to wear after the cataract surgery."

Opening her shoulder bag Shirley pulled out a head scarf. Extending her arm she shook the chiffon silk to its full length.

"The ultimate accessory." Placing the material on her head she wrapped the ends around her neck and turned asking Linda to tie a knot at the back.

"What a lovely colour," Linda said. "Champagne with pink polka dots."

Shirley posed. "How do I look?"

"Glamorous."

Shirley got in the driver's side and shrieked. "My God, it's low. For a second I thought I was going to hit the ground." She put the keys in the ignition. The motor purred like a kitten.

"Wow, that's a quiet engine. I was expecting a roar. They sure did a good job. Worth every cent you paid, Grandma."

Linda and Shirley laughed together like teenagers ready for a rollicking good night. "Clarence always described it as debonair. The only French word he ever spoke."

They laughed again. Linda said, "The billboard said it was, 'The spirited, fun filled mode of travel.'"

"I remember billboard advertising. Isn't it a shame the town got rid of those signs. People don't understand fun anymore."

"Oh, and it was billed as a 'Glide' ride."

"We're going to have fun tonight, Linda."

"I always have fun with you, Shirley." In unison they turned their heads to look one another in what were quickly becoming tear-filled eyes. "What happened to us? Where did the time go?"

"I don't know. But what's the alternative?" Shirley asked.

More shared laughter. "The grave. With Clarence."

"God, we don't want that, do we?"

"You're doing a lot of swearing tonight, Shirley. You better clean up your language before we get those grandkids."

"I'm so glad it's an automatic," Shirley said. "I first learned to drive on a standard gear shift. Remember those? I don't think

I'd know how anymore." Shirley put the car in reverse and backed out of the driveway onto the street.

"So far so good."

"Gee, Linda, this is a thrill. I gotta pay attention, though. The beast is as long as a pick-up truck. Only it's low." Shirley and Linda laughed for the entire drive to Rupert's house.

"Here's my handsome grandson." He was shy around his grandmother and Lily's grandmother which is what he called her. "Hi Grandma. Hi Lily's Grandma."

Linda and Shirley looked at each other and again laughed uproariously. Rupert turned red. Linda and Shirley laughed louder. "Sorry, Rupert. We're not laughing at you. We're just having a ball, that's all."

As soon as Shirley eased the convertible beside the curb in front of her daughter's house Lily came out the front door with her father. She bounced down the sidewalk while Clinton held back letting his daughter get ahead of him. Rupert opened the back passenger door and stood on the grassy verge. "Go get her," Linda said.

Rising on his toes Rupert pranced across the sidewalk. "He's nervous," Linda said.

Shirley put the car in neutral and turned to watch her granddaughter meet Rupert who held her elbow and guided her to the car. They seemed calm together. Then Shirley saw Clinton go inside the house. "Hello Lily. You look beautiful."

Clearly amazed at whose voice she heard behind the elegant large, dark, sunglasses and under a tied chiffon scarf, Lily mumbled, "Grandma, are you driving?"

"Yes, we're going to be in the parade."

"Oh," Lily said stepping into the back seat. Rupert carefully closed the door and ran around to the other side.

Shirley saw Pamela come onto the veranda. Putting the car in 'Drive' Shirley slowly drove down the street keeping her eyes focused on the rear view mirror where she could see the action at the house. By the time she was at the end of the block Pamela was on the street with Clinton. "Your parents are waving at you."

Linda turned around and waved too. She watched the couple as Rupert pinned a corsage on Lily's dress. "Your dress is the colour of your Grandma's scarf."

"It is."

"We match, dear." Shirley focused on driving the convertible and glided the car onto the roundabout at the front of the high school. One of the attendants waved her forward.

"Hi, Mr. Wilson," Rupert and Lily said in unison.

"Good evening. Would you like to lead the parade in this snazzy convertible?"

"We sure would," Shirley said.

"You two will have to sit up on the back of the seats so the people lining the street can get a good look at you."

"We will," Lily said. "When the time comes."

Shirley slowly eased the Oldsmobile past the line of cars until they were in front of everyone. There she stopped and waited.

Lily and Rupert waved and said their hellos to other teenagers who were on tractors, in the back of pickup trucks, and in other convertibles, one a sporty MG. Soon Mr. Wilson was beside them again waving them forward. When the car was in position Mr. Wilson walked to the back of the convertible and, nodding to Lily and Rupert, said, "It's time to climb up to take your position as the head of the prom parade."

Shirley waited for Rupert and Lily to find their perch on the back of the back seat before putting the gear in 'Drive'.

On the main street crowds lined the sidewalk and snapped pictures. The local reporter followed them clicking continually then passed to the car behind them. Shirley kept her eyes on the road and turned at the corner where the police escort directed her to return to the high school.

Linda yelled and waved, "There are your parents." Shirley didn't know if she was talking about her own family or Shirley's, but she wasn't going to turn her head to look. She was determined she was not going to mess up this role. Yet she was flustered by Linda's remark and, rather than ask Linda, she hit the brakes. The sudden stop caused Linda to hit the dashboard whereupon she shrieked. Her friend wasn't the only one who was shrieking. So was her granddaughter. Shirley looked in the rear view mirror to see Lily huddled over Rupert. His legs were in the air, cycling as if he was exercising. Slowly he righted himself. Linda sat back and said, "Shirley, drive the car. We're holding up the parade."

Shirley did as she was told for a change.

At the high school Shirley stopped in front of the main doors and put the gear in 'Park'. Rupert got out first and helped Lily by gallantly extending his hand to her. "Thank you so much, Grandma. That was exciting. I can't believe we got to be at the front in the parade."

"Yes. Thank you both for a swell ride," Rupert said.

"You're welcome," Linda said. "Grandpa Clarence is looking down on you from heaven and he is so proud and happy I got his car fixed up for the best ride of its life."

Both grandmas waved. "Did you see that, Shirley? Rupert is such a gentleman. Any girl will be lucky to marry him."

As Shirley drove forward she looked to her left. All the parking spots were filled.

"What are you doing?" Linda asked.

"Looking for a parking spot." She continued straight ahead where the lot ended. She didn't even have to turn the wheel.

"Why are you parking?"

"Hold on. Let me concentrate."

"Haven't you done enough already?" Linda asked.

"Let's go watch the other couples arrive," Shirley said getting out of the car.

Chapter 9

The Prom Dance

Shirley followed Mr. Wilson into the high school. She turned at the sound of her name. "Shirley. Shirley." It was coming at her as if in a dream. "What is it, Linda?"

"Where are you going?"

"To the prom."

"You can't do that." Linda stood outside on the other side of the door that she was holding open for no one, as the last of the students had trailed into the school gym.

"C'mon," Shirley said nodding her head. "I want to dance."

Linda stepped inside and let the door shut behind her. "Shirley, we've done our duty. We're not invited to the prom dance. It's only for graduating students."

"Let's follow Mr. Wilson in."

"He's the principal."

"So?"

"Shirley, please. Let's go home."

Shirley took Linda's arm holding it under her elbow. "We can help chaperon." She led Linda through the second set of doors and walked down the corridor to the gym where the noise of excited teenagers spilled into the hall.

"There's Michael." Linda sounded troubled.

"Who?"

"Michael Wilson. The Principal. He'll see us."

"Do you know him?"

"Yes. He congratulated us when Rupert was made valedictorian."

Shirley led Linda up to Michael Wilson and asked if he wouldn't mind if they stayed a minute to have a peek at the graduates dancing. He seemed fine with their request. "Sure," he said, "and thank you again for leading the cars in the parade." Then he pointed to the staff who were on duty. "Let those teachers know if you see anything untoward like kids leaving or going to the washroom in packs." Shirley smiled at him and took off her large sunglasses which she only just realized she was still wearing. She placed them on top of her head over the chiffon scarf. Linda told her she was going to start a new fashion trend if she didn't remove that scarf and her sunglasses. "Why, Linda, how can you call it 'that scarf' when earlier you said how glamorous it was. I can pretend to be a fashion icon."

"You're doing enough pretending as it is being here. This is going too far, Shirley." Linda unhooked her arm from Shirley's grasp telling her to stop manhandling her. "Give me your scarf and sunglasses before they fall off your head."

Shirley obliged just as the music started to play and then immediately she turned to a student who was standing behind them like a male wallflower. She asked , "What song is that they're playing?" He said, "It's called, 'Just Dance'."

Shirley announced, "That's exactly what I'm going to do." Before Shirley stepped away from the male wallflower and Linda she heard Lady Gaga sing, "It's alright, just dance." Shirley imitated some students who put their hands over their eyes and then splayed their fingers to peek through as they started marching on the spot. Then they started pumping their fists toward their knees as they lowered their stance which Shirley found hard to do as she couldn't bend that low and her fingers felt stiff from holding the steering wheel earlier. When the group of dancers in front of her started swaying their hips she found she could do that to the beat of the music. Shirley heard more lyrics as Lady Gaga sang, "Don't be afraid, Just dance." At the end of the song Shirley was huffing and puffing.

"That's it then," Linda said when Shirley returned to her side. "Let's go before you faint."

"Wait until I catch my breath," Shirley said. She stood beside Linda swaying to the next few songs that had the same beat as the first song. She looked across the dance floor to see if she could spot Lily and Rupert but the mass of writhing bodies looked like intertwined branches of thick vines that were impenetrable. At once Shirley remembered the road to Dougie Nicholl's place and she felt claustrophobic until she willed herself to trace the car route in her mind to when they came to the clearing. The music mirrored her calmness. Again she turned to the wall flower. "This music is different. It's slower."

"Yes," he said. "It's called 'Silence'."

"Well how can a song be called 'Silence'?"

"It's from Karma by Sarah McLachlan."

"She's Canadian, isn't she?"

The youth nodded.

"Linda," Shirley said eager to keep her friend by her side. "This wonderful song is being sung by a Canadian. Listen." After a couple of minutes of instrumental guitar Sarah McLachlan's distinct voice started singing soft lyrics. After a couple of more minutes her voice grew more distinct and Shirley heard phrases like 'Sense of wonder' and 'I believe'.

"Well," Linda said, "I didn't expect to hear hymn-like lyrics in a popular dance song."

Shirley sang, "Heaven knows a sense of wonder I wanted to believe In this sadness I believe I have seen it."

"I like how they danced to that tune. That's more like we used to dance although they're still not in couples. I don't understand. They make such a big deal about having a date and then they dance in a mob instead of with their partner."

"Listen, I think this next song is in French."

"Yes," the boy behind them piped up to confirm that what they were hearing was French. "Ella Elle l'a." He started singing along as were most of the students on the dance floor, but unlike him, they were swaying to the music with their hands on their hips.

"They know the words because they've learned French," Shirley said. "We were never taught French." She, too, put her fists on her hips which she could not feel through the fat on them and started swaying to the music feeling very nostalgic for her past. She grabbed the arm of the youth beside her and held him close as she led him in step to the music. "This is more like it."

The local reporter appeared in front of her and snapped her picture.

Linda grabbed Shirley's arm and pulled her away from the young lad. "Let's get out of here."

Chapter 10

At the Clubhouse

On Sunday after church six couples gathered at the golf course for the Father's Day Special. The club house was built in a traditional park-like setting with an imposing grouping of mature trees along the driveway. The stone house that served as the Dellport club house originally had the name Stoneview and it was designed with a west facing view across the lake. The original builder placed an orangery on the south side which added to the harmony of the place with its setting.

Tony sat beside Ramsey Reisch, his friend and former chief of police. They both ordered a Clubhouse Sandwich. "I bet you're glad you don't have the pressures of policing any more?"

"You can say that again. And I have a great pension."

"That's more than I can say."

"C'mon. You can't fool me, Tony. You're loaded, but I won't hold it against you." Ramsey chuckled.

Tony asked Ramsey quietly, "Christopher James wants to put my name forward to run for council. Do you think this brouhaha around Clinton has died down enough that I can run?"

"Oh, sure. Go for it, Tony. I'll back you."

"Thanks. So much for retirement, eh? " Tony said.

"Well let me ask you about funding retirement since you

brought up the topic. Recently I've seen the value of my mutual funds decline. Will they go into free-fall, I wonder?" Ramsey asked.

"I know others in the same boat but I would advise switching all your funds to guaranteed investment securities."

Ramsey said, "But when the funds regain their value guys like you will be left in the lurch."

"Then switch them back when you can buy them cheap," Tony advised.

"For crying out loud, can't I wait out the risks. What good investment doesn't involve risk? Bunch of softies. Meet me here this time next year and I'll be the one laughing all the way to the bank."

Tony folded his arms across his chest and nodded in agreement. He looked out the window at the flourishing greens, the blossoming gardens along the perimeter, and beyond to the lake that was a Caribbean blue on this fine day. This was the good life. Why spoil it? He'd been playing this course since he was a boy when he came with his father. Here's to you Dad, Tony thought. Elmo Palmer had been a good mentor. When Tony had returned from completing his undergraduate degree in business his father had suggested that he take over the hardware store. It turned out to have been a good long term investment. Of course, the terms were generous. Same terms he would have offered Johnny if the boy hadn't disappeared.

Yes indeed, Tony thought. It was a fitting place to be on Father's Day. Then he had an idea. Dellport Window Cleaners had recently cleaned all the windows here. He used the same firm at his house to clean his windows. They came twice a year, once in the spring and again later in the fall. Len, the owner, always said those were his busy seasons. Come the summer he laid off his workers or sent them on holiday. One of those idle window washers could clean his floors, Tony now thought. If someone can clean windows Tony figured he could clean his house. Shirley and he were finding it hard to keep up with the cleaning since Felicia had left. It now seemed she'd be gone for the whole summer if not for good so it would be prudent to get some help.

Shirley broke his reverie by reminding him that they were hosting a barbecue later so maybe he shouldn't eat the whole sandwich. Tony looked down at the plate that the waiter placed on the table in front of him and thought of a cost saving measure. He turned to Ramsey. "Maybe we could ask the kitchen to serve senior portions thereby reducing costs."

"You mean charge the same amount for less food?"

"Yes, raise the price of the regular portion and make the regular price the cost of the smaller, senior portion. The kitchen reported there's a lot of food waste." Both Tony and Ramsey served on the board at the golf course. Just like them the place was feeling financially squeezed. Memberships were down. People no longer wanted to join a club like theirs and play on the same holes every time they went golfing. Nowadays they liked to try other courses and take holidays abroad to play elsewhere. Gone was any sense of loyalty to a place or the desire to make long-lasting friendships. Ramsey and he knew one another from childhood. They'd gone through school together. They were good buddies. They'd supported each other through marriage and raising families. They shared concerns about the well-being of the community where they'd resided all their lives. How could they keep the golf course afloat? People their age were quitting the game or passing away.

Ramsey wiped his mouth after eating one half of his

sandwich and reached for the glass of water at the top of his place mat. His hand shook when he returned the half empty glass. "Boy, I was thirsty," he said. "I've been thinking we need to make a proposal to the board to seek investors."

"Like offer shares?"

"Well, something. We need to talk about this with the board members."

"Good idea, Ramsey. You have my support." Tony picked up his fork and stabbed a fry. "I'd better eat these before my wife tells me I shouldn't."

"They'd go soggy if you tried to take them home."

"Wasn't that part of the unexpected expenditures that the kitchen reported? The cost of those containers to people who wanted to take home their left-overs?"

"Not to mention the cost to the environment, but best not to go down that road or the fringe element will bring up the cost of pesticides. Some people are real spoiled sports."

"You mean the cost of replacing pesticides?"

"Some people would like to shut us down."

"Over my dead body."

"Amen."

Chapter 11

Father's Day

Tony was putting on his chef's apron when the family arrived. Pamela kissed his cheek and commented that he was wearing his present from last year. "It's always hard to know what to get you," she said. "Happy Father's Day."

"Hi Grandpa," Lily said and she, too, kissed his cheek. "Happy Grandfather's Day."

Clinton and Tim hauled a large parcel through the door. Given the difference in strength between father and son the box was lopsided. "Careful," Clinton said when they dropped it on the floor. Then he closed the door behind him.

"Happy Father's Day to you, Clinton," Tony said.

"Thank you. It's been quite the morning."

"He got breakfast in bed," Pamela said. "Our children are good chefs. They just don't understand how dishwashers work." She ran her fingers through her hair under the nape of her neck as if trying to relieve her head of the heat generated by the weather and her family.

"Something got caught in the drain and dad had to pull it all apart."

"Not your fault, Tim."

"Come in, come in you all," Shirley called from the back. "We're outside."

"Strictly speaking she means she's outside," Lily said.

"Don't be mean to your grandma after she was so nice to you on your graduation."

"I'm not being mean. I'm just stating a fact." Lily bit her bottom lip. She was feeling a little defensive. On no account did she ever wish to be mean.

"Did you hear, Dad? Mom drove Lily and Rupert to the prom in a classy convertible."

"I did hear something about that," Tony said turning and leading his step family outside.

Shirley was standing on the deck and Pamela went over to her and gave her a kiss on the cheek. "Oh, why am I being treated to a kiss? It's not Mother's Day," Shirley said.

Lily also kissed Shirley on the cheek. "Thanks again for driving me and Rupert to the prom."

"Rupert and me," Tim said correcting her. "Strictly speaking."

"Get a life, Tim."

"Tim has some good news, don't you mister," Clinton said.

"'What's that?" Shirley asked. She sat down on the lounge chair and stretched her legs along the length of the cushioned seat. She had short legs which didn't reach the full length of the chaise lounge. Shirley had always felt self-conscious about them but now she felt worse because they had turned into stumps and the skin along her limbs was turning to flab. No more muscle. Picking up her large sunglasses from the side table she placed them on her head and smiled at her grandson. He told her about the top prize he'd won for his essay on the food crisis in Haiti. "What food crisis?" she asked.

Tim said, "There were food riots in April because of the shortage of food on the island and sky-rocketing prices."

"How awful," Shirley said. "I can't imagine not having enough food to eat."

"I'd like to read your essay." Tony picked up a tool from under the barbecue and started scraping the grill.

"Sure, Grandpa. I'll bring it over next week."

"Grandma, you were wearing those sunglasses when you drove us."

"I sure was, dear."

"Grandpa, did you see her? She looked so glamorous. Everybody said so. They couldn't believe you're my Grandma. They thought you were my mother or sister."

"It was that silk scarf," Pamela said. "All we could see was you behind the wheel wearing those large sunglasses with that polka dot scarf around your head. You looked like Grace Kelly." She lightly touched her neck wondering about the feel of silk against her skin.

"Princess for a day," Shirley said.

"What can I get you to drink?" Tony asked returning the scraper to the metal shelf below the grill and rubbing his palms together.

After taking orders Pamela said she would come inside to help.

"We should all go inside," Clinton said. "We need to go inside to open the present. There's no point hauling it out here."

They went into the kitchen then took their drinks to the front hall where Tony proceeded to unwrap the large box. "How did you get this here?"

"We drove over in my pickup," Clinton said.

The wrapping paper was off and the cardboard flaps lifted when they heard a knock at the door. "Who could that be?" Shirley asked. Since she was the person standing closest to the front door she opened it.

"Hi Mom."

Everyone turned when they heard Johnny's voice. Shirley shrieked and gave her son a hug. Pushing him to arm's length she looked around him to the car parked on the street. "How did you know we were here?" Without waiting for an answer she asked, "Where's your bags? You can stay in your old room."

"Just for the night."

"Well, well, well. The prodigal returns." Clinton extended his hand in greeting.

Dodging behind her family Pamela was at his side in an instant. After hugging him she turned to her children. "Say hello to your Uncle Johnny."

"Hey, I wouldn't have recognized them if I'd met them on the street. You're all grown up, Lily." Awkwardly he reached over to give his niece a quick hug before extending his hand to Tim. "Nice to see you, buddy."

"Ditto," Tim said.

"Welcome home." Tony's head started shaking and the skin on his high forehead was twitching. Was he angry? Was he happy? He hadn't seen his son for two years. Mostly he felt relieved. His nervous ticks were physical signs of tension letting go.

"Thanks, Dad."

"But you're only staying one night?" Shirley asked.

"'Fraid so."

"Let's make this a special day, then, shall we?" Tony said drawing his family's attention back to the task at hand. "So what do we have in here?" First he pulled out a manual and read, "Easy push lawnmower."

"We got it at the Honda dealership."

"It was on special," Tim said, adding more to his mother's explanation than was needed.

"Since you're retired and spending more time in the garden," Clinton said, "we thought you could use it."

"I'll say," Shirley said. "He was out there at 5 o'clock this morning."

"Let's be fair. I wasn't cutting the grass at that hour. I know better than to start up that noisy mower and wake the neighbours."

"I can take that noisy monster off your hands and try to fix it."

"Thank you, Clinton, and thank you everybody. This is perfect for me since I hate riding lawnmowers," Tony said. "It seems everybody on the street has one of those."

"I didn't come empty handed," Johnny said pulling an envelope from his pant pocket.

"It looks like a money card," Tim said.

Opening it Tony said, "It is. Look at these." He pulled two old paper bills from the card and waved them in front of his family. "From 1945. The year I was born."

"Wow, they're ancient. They must be valuable." Tim took one and turned it over to read the inscription.

"What does that make me?" Tony laughed before offering his son a drink.

"Just a pop, Dad."

"You have changed," Clinton said.

There was an awkward moment in the hall before Tony piped up, "We're all a little stunned, Johnny. It's just like you to show up unannounced, but you're always welcome. You know that, don't you? This is your home."

"Of course. I'm off the booze, you'll be glad to hear."

"I'm just bursting to ask you questions."

"You ask too many questions, Mom."

"I know. I haven't changed, but either have you. Even if you're not drinking."

"Yep, we'd recognize you anywhere," Clinton said.

"C'mon," Shirley said impatiently.

The family marched outside and took up chairs while Tony cooked on the barbecue. Lily and Tim crowded around their Uncle Johnny who placed a chair beside his mother's lounge chair. He asked them what they'd been up to lately. Lily relayed how she was finished school and going to university in the fall. Tim said he was still in school until the end of the month. Pamela piped up that Mom had driven Lily to the prom and described the car and the parade.

"I'm surprised you didn't crash the dance," Johnny said.

"She did," Clinton said.

"Don't be unfair," Shirley said. "Tim, dear, bring over that bowl of chips we can all share." While she waited for her grandson she started thinking how perceptive her son was, which got her thinking about what a disappointment he was not being around to take over the hardware store from his dad or having a permanent girlfriend and settling down. She knew better than to mention any of this because they had been over it a thousand times and Tony made it clear that the family was to accept Johnny on his own terms which only left her in the dark about what he'd been up to these past two years.

When the bugs arrived at dusk they retreated back indoors.

Pamela sat in the front room with her brother sipping decaf coffee. He told her how great her kids were. "Only they bicker," she said.

"That's normal."

"Not for us. I was never mean to you, was I?"

"No, you weren't. Maybe that was part of my problem. I never had to stick up for myself."

"Unfair," Pamela said.

Johnny smiled. "Sorry, Pamela. I don't blame you. I take full responsibility for my errant ways. By the way, where's Felicia? I'd like to see her."

"Funny you should ask," Pamela said before proceeding to tell him the whole story. At the conclusion she cautioned, "Mum's the word. No one but the adults know the whole truth. As I said, Dougie Nicholl took the rap."

"Is Mom getting crazy in her old age? Though driving in the parade with Linda Leach in an antique car sounds like just the kind of thing she'd do."

Just then Shirley poked her head around the door. "More coffee?"

"No thanks, Mom."

Shirley stepped into the room. In a conspiratorial voice she addressed her son saying he must consider staying long enough to attend Lily's graduation ceremony. "The rest of the family will be there and don't you want to show her how proud you are of her?"

"I think she knows I'm proud of her without me sitting through some ceremony especially since I never attended my own."

Shirley kept her voice low saying that he would be conspicuous in his absence and emphasizing again that everyone would be there in support.

"I think enough people around town have already seen me."

"What do you mean by that?" Shirley asked.

"We should be going now," Pamela said.

Shirley shook off her secretive attitude and said, "First come and join us in the kitchen. Johnny, you'll want to hear the conversation the boys are having. Tim and Grandpa and Clinton are talking about the state of the economy. It all started with Haiti and Tim telling us about his essay. It's gone way over my head but I still think we should do something about the situation."

"Like what?" Pamela asked with a hint of warning in her voice.

"Like hold a demonstration," Shirley said spinning on her heels and leaving the room.

Johnny looked at the empty doorway then back at Pamela. He waved his hand in the direction of his departed mother.

"What's she up to?"

"She's always up to something," Pamela said. "Like driving in the prom parade like the kids."

"Remember how Auntie Jane always told us about being crowned the Queen of the Prom."

"It's good we don't engage in such sexist behaviour anymore."

"I thought it was to prove she was pretty even though she wasn't into boys."

"Maybe." Pamela leaned in closer and put her hand on Johnny's knee. "Can you keep a secret?"

"Sure. I'm gone tomorrow. No one to tell."

She shared with him what she was doing to try to track down her birth father.

"Good for you," Johnny said. "It's time we set the record straight about your real dad."

"Mom's determined to keep him in the shadow of my life. She insists he's the bad guy in her life. But just because they were young once doesn't make him bad."

"I agree. They were both young once. How come she's not labeled bad?"

"I don't think we want to answer that question."

"Never mind. I can help you." Then he told her his secret.

In a time of extreme indecision either way is a gamble but Pamela was now decisive. Having her half brother's support served to confirm that she was doing the right thing by her family. "Thank you, Johnny. I can't tell you how hard it's been for me to go down this path. There are agencies I could use but I wanted to do this on my own. I really don't want to have to explain myself to Mom and if I took the formal route they would contact her. I've learned enough in my line of work to figure out how these things are done. Clinton has been very supportive, too."

"He's a good guy."

"Your secret is safe with me."

"Mom can never know. She'd hit the roof."

"Maybe not. To give her credit, she just wants to know that you are safe. All mothers feel like that, even when their children are grown. I know Dad doesn't say much but I'm sure he feels the same way. He is a parent, too."

"I know, I know. I put them both through the ringer. Sometime this summer maybe you can sneak away and come and visit me? You'd like it there. Bring the family. Have a holiday."

"Maybe we will."

With that they rose and joined their family in the kitchen.

Chapter 12

Strumming on the Banjo

At The Bletch on Wednesday Paolo found the members of the banjo group in a huddle at the end of a table talking loudly. Standing on the fringe he peeked over someone's shoulder to see what all the fuss was. There was a double spread of pages from the local newspaper that showed pictures taken of the prom parade and the graduates at the high school. It was a special insert on glossy paper. The first picture at the top of the page showed Shirley behind the wheel of the Oldsmobile convertible with Lily and Rupert sitting high in the back waving to the crowd. Paolo recognized the faces of many of the other teenagers from around town and from the store. He also remembered when Patrick was in the same prom parade. At the time Paolo and Felicia thought the event was similar to some of the rituals they enjoyed in their culture. Now it made him homesick to look at these public displays of a local celebration but what caught his eye was the last one on the page, the photograph on the bottom. It was a picture of Shirley dancing.

Paolo sat down. He tried to gather his thoughts but an eerie image from ancient memory sprung to his mind, a picture of a dancing saurian, the hybrid creature part lizard, part human. That is what he took from that last glossy photo. In this transfixed state he continued to listen to the discussion about what the girls wore and who they were dating. Someone pointed out that Lily Croft was Shirley Palmer's granddaughter. Then another voice piped in that she was also Clinton Croft's daughter. There was much hilarity over those revelations. One player knew all about Linda Leach's classy antique car. That got the group started on what vehicles were in the parade. The final word went to the old woman dancing and how she must have crashed the prom after driving in the parade. They closed the newspaper but talk continued, mostly along the lines of salacious speculation which developed into an air of curiosity and soon the banjo players put Shirley under a microscope. In the past neighbours had been at best indifferent and at worst asked pointed questions about her behaviour. Now they made her accountable for her actions because she had drawn attention to herself with that picture published in the local newspaper. She wasn't just a helpful driver for their young. Shirley Palmer was a door crasher. A dancer.

No one was minding their own business except Paolo who remained unnoticed. Someone had much to say about the past when Shirley returned to town with her little girl. That was when she married Anthony Palmer. They regarded that whole affair with suspicion. Someone made a wink-and-nudge joke about Shirley having a baby before she got married.

"Remember how she left Dellport before graduating to work up north at her uncle's resort?"

"Sure do. I think that's what killed her mother. The shame of it all."

"Why? Was the uncle the father?"

"No, no. She got knocked up by some guy and married him, but he was a loser."

"So she's been married twice?"

"The son was back in town on the weekend. Johnny."

"He was? Haven't seen him in a donkey's age."

Finally one of the banjo players saw Paolo sitting quietly on the fringe and greeted him. Then everyone turned. They all had meaningful smiles pasted on their faces, as if they were somehow superior to him, when in fact they were all socially inept. Paolo thought how these people who ridiculed others were making up for their own failures. There were plenty of people like them in Dellport.

Suddenly Brenda Bain appeared dressed for the occasion in a loose, printed blouse, flared, dark skirt, and leather cowboy boots. "Sorry, I'm late," she said, but before she could sit down, someone suggested they move outside to the patio. Amid the clamour of picking up their banjos Brenda leaned into Paolo and whispered, "Is it something I said?"

"No," Paolo said reassuring her. He pointed to the newspaper still spread across the end of the table. "Something they said."

Brenda took a long look at the paper before heading out the door behind Paolo. "You must fill me in later."

There was a view of the lake from the patio that caught Paolo's attention. This evening the light on the lake was gold, a colour he'd never before associated with the large body of water called Lake Huron after the indigenous tribe of natives who once inhabited these shores. Gold was not a precious metal found anywhere near here but it was found near his home. It was revered by his ancestors and claimed by others who discovered it when they stumbled upon the shores where his ancestors lived. The small lakes there reflected gold in shallow bed rock under water. Lake Huron was a huge body of water that changed colour all day long and into the night. The sun radiated across its surface gleaming white and silver. Sometimes clouds shadowed the light turning it dark grey and deep blue. Often Felicia and he would take an evening stroll along the shore and remark to each other about what they saw. They walked everywhere, had never owned a car, not needing one where they lived in town close to where they worked. Still their son, Patrick, got his driver's license and sometimes drove his friends' cars, especially if they'd been drinking and he hadn't. He never aspired to owning a car. Patrick was sensible in that way.

Many of the players sat around one table. A few players stood on the lower, wide stair that led from the building down to the patio. They positioned themselves as if they were setting up on stage. After announcing that they had been rehearsing on their tenor banjos, the three seated on the step played a tune called "12th Street Rag". Len who ran the Dellport Window Washers business took the solo lead while the other two strummed the chords of the refrain.

Much applause followed, not only from the banjo group, but also the regulars who were sitting outside joined in to show their appreciation.

"I've been practicing some Scottish banjo music," Paolo said. Len asked him if he was confused about his identity. Was he Mexican or Scottish? Paolo didn't laugh along with the others. He just started strumming his solo tune that he'd been practicing at home during the lonely evening hours. At the end Brenda put her hands together and clapped. The others joined her with polite applause.

Later, on the drive home with Brenda, Paolo said, "Felicia is still in Vancouver. She doesn't want to come home. If I told her about Shirley's latest antics at the prom she would never want to return to Dellport, especially since the whole town was talking about it. Unlike most people in this town, Felicia always minded her own business."

Brenda nodded. "There's too much small talk, especially of the kind that puts down others."

"Felicia is happy to work for generous people, but now everything has come crashing down on her head. She begin to feel threatened."

"I can understand how everything can suddenly change for someone in her position." Brenda asked, "Are you going to go out west?"

"I guess I must." He didn't say how much he missed her.

"Yes, you should. Can you get time off work?"

Paolo explained how he always took holidays in July because the supermarket could hire students to stock the produce department shelves. He did not share with Brenda that holidays never included travel to distant places because they did not have the money for such expensive trips. Yet out of politeness he thanked her for talking to him about it.

Although he felt emotionally exhausted when he entered his house and wanted nothing more than his bed, he picked up the phone and dialed the west coast. He shared his desire with Felicia saying how much he missed her and Patrick. "I wish I could see you in person, not just on Skype. I'm going to feel really lonely on my holidays being on my own here. I told my boss that I didn't need to take holidays this year but Max said that he'd already lined up students to do my job. The store gets busy in the summer and he has three students to train. Imagine, three students to do my job?"

After he got into bed Felicia called back. "Roberto wants you to come to visit next month and he'll arrange a plane ticket."

Paolo objected to having his brother-in-law pay. "That's so expensive. I can't let Rob spend so much money on me. He's been generous already."

Felicia reassured him. "My brother will use points so don't fuss because Roberto has more points than he can ever use in a lifetime."

Paolo doubted that, but he was too tired to argue and too happy at the prospect of seeing his family to object to the generosity shown him. "I'm so happy I can come to join you there."

Chapter 13

Dealing the Cards

On Thursday Shirley drove Linda to bridge. As soon as she got into the car Linda asked if Shirley had seen the pictures in the local paper. That question started Shirley off with a full blown description of how her daughter had phoned yesterday. "Pamela accused me of having crashed the prom dance. Only last week she'd been so grateful that we'd driven Lily and Rupert in the prom parade. Now she's full of accusations. I made it very clear to Pamela that we did not crash the dance, that we were not even on the dance floor but standing on the sidelines, that we were there talking to the principal, Michael Wilson."

Linda remained quiet, choosing to simply listen. Shirley sounded very indignant. Linda did not counter anything Shirley said, especially her claims about how they happened to be present at the prom dance or who they talked to while standing inside the gym. When they pulled into the driveway Shirley was calm. Her rant about Pamela's treatment of her over she settled her energies and composed herself. They walked decorously up to the front door. The house was a grand house, bigger even than Shirley's house. Linda always felt she needed to apologize when it was her turn to host because her house was ordinary, a two bedroom bungalow. She set the card table up in the middle of the living room to play bridge. Jane actually had a games room behind the formal living room. This was the original Palmer residence which Jane had inherited when their parents died. Anthony acquired full interest in the business and Jane the residence.

When Jane greeted them at the door she led them through the long room that had a semicircular bank of upholstered seats below the window with two separate sitting areas that filled the length of the room. Barbara had lived with Jane for years under the guise that Jane needed the company in her spacious abode. Barbara lived on the third floor in a totally separate apartment reached by the back stairs off the kitchen.

There was a door to the kitchen off the games room and Barbara was there filling the kettle. When she turned off the water she came into the room and the first thing she said was, "I saw the pictures of the two of you in the local paper."

Even with Barbara and Jane, Linda remained mute. What was the point? Everyone had formed their own opinions about what the two of them were doing at the prom dance and no amount of counter logic would change anyone's minds.

By the time Shirley told what was now 'their' story for the third or fourth time (to Pamela, Tony, Linda and now Barbara and Jane), she was as neutral and dismissive as only Shirley could be when faced with major hysteria. So, as the cards were being dealt and play began, the topic expanded to sharing many details on what the women thought of the different dresses and vehicles shown in the newspaper spread. "I'm glad the pictures were in colour," Linda said. "I know Clarence was looking down from Heaven and was proud of his Olds. It was gleaming."

"Lily's dress was beautiful," Jane said, "but what about the others, like that awful ruby one? As bad as wearing black. And it was short."

"I know," Barbara said. "I think Lily had on the prettiest dress at the prom. I don't understand girls. Where are their mothers? Does everyone in this town have bad taste?"

"Yes," Jane said, "which is why the clothing store downtown is closing."

"It is?" Linda asked.

"You mean Adele's?" Shirley asked.

"The same. Rumour has it. After sixty years in business."

"But that's where Lily bought her prom dress and accessories."

"That explains why it was so beautiful and tasteful. You don't get clothes like that anywhere else. Not in this town."

"It's those box stores. They ruin it for the businesses downtown." Shirley said adding that she had been a loyal customer to Adele's. At least since being married to Tony she was because she could afford to be. She could never afford to shop there when she lived with her mother when growing up or when she returned with Pamela. When growing up her mother sewed her clothes and when she had a toddler they shopped at discount stores, sometimes second hand shops, or accepted hand-me-downs.

"I agree. Big box stores do ruin the retail trade," Barbara said. "And they only stock clothes for the young and tasteless. Where will we shop now?"

"We'll have to drive all the way to London," Jane said.

"We will. I'll drive," Shirley said. "We can make it a seasonal outing."

"Four times a year," Jane said, laying down her winning cards and marking the score.

"Well look at you."

"I've been looking at you, Shirley. Are you letting your hair grow?" Jane asked.

"I am. What do you think?" Shirley patted the back of her head.

"I think it suits you."

After dealing another hand Shirley said, "At least we have plenty of food to eat."

"Of course we have food," Babara said, not disguising her exasperation with Shirley's wayward remark. "We weren't born during the depression."

"Food is getting more expensive," Linda said, recognizing that Shirley wasn't being perverse. "At least, that's what I've found."

"I hadn't noticed," Barbara said wrinkling her nose as she spread her cards.

"Of course you haven't noticed," Jane said. "You don't do the shopping. I do."

"Then tell me. Is it more expensive?" Barbara asked turning to Jane then looking over at Linda.

Now who's being perverse, Linda thought. "If you're living on a fixed income like me and keeping to a budget you'd soon see that everything is going up in price."

"It's way more expensive in Haiti and what's more, they don't even have any food," Shirley said.

"What's Haiti got to do with us?" Babara asked. Clearly she was growing disgruntled.

"This is what Tim says," Shirley began.

"Tim?" Barbara asked.

"Tim," Jane said. "You know, my nephew, Tim."

"My grandson."

"How old is he now?" Barbara asked.

"He's turning thirteen this summer," Shirley said.

"A teenager already," Barbara said. "Sure to be trouble."

"Tim's a sensible boy," Shirley said. "He's no trouble."

"You'd say that. You're his grandmother."

"Listen to me, Barbara," Shirley said, sounding forceful. She then proceeded to tell them about Tim's essay on the food riots in Haiti. "We need to do something," she concluded.

"We do?" Babara asked.

"Like what?" Linda asked.

"I think we need to hold a demonstration."

"Where would we do that?" Jane asked, sounding doubtful. "I agree Tim is a mature boy for his age and I'm sure he makes a good case but did he actually suggest we hold a demonstration?"

"I've never demonstrated about anything in my life," Linda said with a morsel of regret.

"Why would we? We were born after the depression and the war." Barbara slammed a card down and raised her eyebrows challenging anyone to trump her lead.

"This is my idea," Shirley said completely ignoring Barbara's winning hand and Jane's earlier question. Shirley explained her plan and, before they finished playing cards, Shirley had convinced them about the need for a rally in front of the local supermarket.

"We can't organize it too soon," Linda said. "We don't want to interrupt school."

"I thought that was the whole point," Barbara said. "To cause a disruption."

"But not during the end of school term," Jane said. "I agree with Linda. We don't want to appear irresponsible."

"No," Linda said. "They're writing exams now."

"Haven't they finished writing exams? It's the end of June." Barbara again raised her eyebrows to get a good look at what was still in her hand.

"I guess so. Tonight is the graduation ceremony at the high school. Are you going, Shirley?"

"Yes, Linda. You, too?"

"Oh I wouldn't miss it for the world."

"We can do it in July," Shirley said, full of the spirit of independence. She knew enough to go along with Jane and Linda who thought there was nothing wrong with having to curtail important activities to study for exams. They thought there was something good about having a limited life. Shirley knew they still judged her for having left school before completing her year. They all knew she'd failed more than once. They all knew she'd been encouraged by Tony to complete what she'd missed when first married, before Johnny was born. Still she was glad to go to the formal graduation ceremonies. Tonight would be the perfect opportunity to talk to Tim but she thought it best to caution her bridge partners. "Keep this under your hat for now."

Chapter 14

Graduation

When Pamela went to Dellport High School back in the 1980s it was a brand new building. Now here she was decades later walking through the front doors to attend her daughter's graduation on the very spot where she herself had graduated. She felt a buzz of excitement. Everything looked the same: the stackable chairs of molded plywood set up on the gym floor, the stage at the opposite end from the doors where the lectern stood, the high ceiling festooned with balloons and paper ribbon. Yet it could only be the same in her memory. Surely these chairs weren't the same ones from her days. On closer examination the slats covering the stage floor were cracked and looked like they should be replaced. Come to think of it she didn't remember there being decorations. In her day graduation was taken more sternly, less festively, more formally. Maybe the stage got decorated. Maybe it was so dark in the gym she couldn't see the decorations or maybe it was her memory that was dark. Besides how did they get balloons and bunting up there? They must have had help from the caretakers. For sure the ventilation was the same as it was in her day. There was still no air conditioning. Pamela saw that some people had brought fans and were already waving them in front of their sweaty faces.

She jostled with Tim at her side to secure a row of five chairs. They were saving places for Clinton who was parking the car and for her parents who were to meet them inside the school. When Clinton arrived she moved over one chair so he was sitting between her and Tim who remained standing looking back at the entrance to watch for his grandparents. When he saw them he motioned like a sentinel waving flag signals on board a navy ship. As soon Shirley reached them she waved across the room to her friend Linda Leach before sitting next to Tim. Tony sat at the end of the row and immediately turned around to speak to a golf buddy who was sitting directly behind him. Pamela forgot his name but recognized his face. It was just like her parents to turn every event into a community visit. The school auditorium and the clubhouse were treated like extensions of their house.

The acoustics were so terrible Pamela was feeling dizzy from the echo. Stale air, poor sound, inattentive family. Pamela reminded herself to be brave for the sake of her daughter. It was her night.

Pamela passed copies of the programme down the row thinking she was being a dutiful mother as well as a messenger. She wanted to say out loud to her parents to pay attention to the programme instead of engaging everyone in the room because the reason they were gathered together was for a member of the family but she kept silent and simply prayed they would all turn their attention to the evening's festivities when things got underway. With unusual flourish Pamela opened her remaining copy to read the order of the night's proceedings. Rupert Leach was listed as the valedictorian. Pamela knew they would see Lily on stage many times, not just to receive her graduation diploma, but also her Honours Award, something the school board had recently reintroduced. It came as a result of many changes made to the curriculum by the government.

Finally people came on stage, and the master of ceremonies asked the audience to stand for the national anthem. That was followed by a welcome speech from Principal Michael Wilson. Various people on stage stood to make many presentations for awards including the honours students. Pamela beamed when Lily crossed the stage and Clinton clutched her knee to indicate how proud he was too.

Then Pamela found her mind wandering. She was thinking about her father, her real father, her birth father. His name was Monty Caragiale, the man her mother discouraged her from knowing. The man who was legitimately her father. The man her mother thought was some monster. Yet he couldn't have always been a monster otherwise why would her mother have fallen for him? He was proving hard to track but not impossible. Pamela was learning to play sleuth. It was hard going since she didn't bear his name but that didn't matter to Pamela or the authorities. She wondered if her mother had ever taken on his name. Had she once been Shirley Caragiale, even for a brief time? Pamela was curious about that but not so curious she would dare to ask her mother. Such a question would cause suspicion. Without any definite answers Pamela continued to speculate. Had her mother become Shirley Caragiale after being Shirley Anne Montgomery and before becoming Shirley Palmer? Was she attracted to him because his first name was her surname? Had they joked about that when they met? There were so many stories about them and her conception that Pamela did not know. He was long gone but Pamela was getting closer and knew he must still be alive and was not out of reach.

Finally, the procession of all the graduates entered the stage to receive their diplomas. Afterwards Rupert faced a challenging audience when he gave his valedictorian speech but he was so articulate everyone paid rapt attention. While clapping Pamela held on to his forewarning that in the face of a looming economic crisis they would prosper, to his prediction that in the face of global challenges they would unite, and in the face of threatening environmental changes they would prove themselves to be innovators.

When it was over, Clinton reached under his chair and pulled out the bouquet of flowers he'd brought for his daughter. Together they waited for Lily to find them through the crowd. Pamela felt they were like teenagers themselves, shaping up to congratulate their daughter who was at the end of her teenage years, about to embark on adulthood. Their children's welfare was always their paramount consideration. They could not be faulted as parents, yet it seemed to her that they'd found that course through default. It was as natural as breathing.

Then Lily was in front of them and Clinton handed over the flowers and gave her a big hug. Pamela followed saying she hoped there would be many more occasions to shower her with flower blossoms. Lily broke away with smiling eyes and turned to her grandfather. After embracing him she asked, "Where are Tim and Grandma? I saw them sitting beside you."

Together they searched the crowded room. "There they are," Pamela said, gesturing. "Talking to some of Tim's friends." She felt reassured by the sight. Seeing the different generations together on this evening in June demonstrated they were a supportive family unit. Her mother took a keen interest in the well being of her grandchildren and her friend's grandchildren. You could not fault her for that.

Chapter 15

The Golf Tournament

Tony invited the new chief of police and his wife to join them for the mixed golf tournament held on Sunday, June 29. Usually they played with Ramsey Reisch and his wife, Rose, but, as he explained to Shirley, he had promised the new chief that he would introduce him to the locals. She recognized what he implied by 'promise'. This was a gesture to return the favour for releasing Clinton. Shirley took it upon herself to smooth any hard feelings Rose might have by explaining to her over the phone that Tony wanted the members to get to know the new chief. "You will forgive us for not following tradition."

"Of course, what are friends for?"

On hearing Rose's agreeable response Shirley breathed a sigh of relief. Although she felt a loyalty to Clinton she wasn't prepared to sacrifice their friendship with Ramsey and Rose by covering up for him. Clearly friendship and fidelity and forgiveness were all part and parcel of the same thread that kept people together. "As well," Shirley added, "Albert Schroeder has chosen not to move to town because his wife wants to remain close to her family."

"We can all understand that sentiment," Rose said in empathy.

More relief. Shirley could trust Rose and, as far as Shirley was concerned, Tony. The golf club couldn't have timed the tournament better. She had some questions for the new chief. Now was the time to plan, to set her ideas into motion and to do some background research of her own.

Although cloudy, Sunday proved a good day for playing golf. The rain remained south of them and the storms to the east. The parking lot at the gold club was full so Tony dropped Shirley off at the front door to park his car in the overflow lot. While waiting, Shirley played the role of chatelaine, greeting everyone she knew as if they were her personal guests. An unfamiliar couple arrived and stood inside the door. Albert Shroeder turned to the animated Shirley when there was a lull in the stream of people arriving and introduced himself. "You must be Shirley, Tony's wife."

"I am. Glad to meet you."

"This is my wife, Hilda."

Shirley thought he seemed a jaunty character. He was dressed like a golf pro in long summer pants with a collared shirt that showed a Nike label. Most of the men at the club wore shorts and socks that gave them tans on their knees. Most of the members, male and female, wore collared shirts with the Dellport Golf & Country Club logo displayed on the pocket. That's what Shirley was wearing with a skort, a tasteful piece of attire that combined shorts with a skirt. Hilda was wearing a sleeveless top with a collarless neckline and matching shorts. Maybe the couple didn't belong to a golf club? Abandoning small talk, Shirley cut to the chase. "So what do you think of public demonstrations, Albert?"

"Well," Albert said looking at her curiously. "You mean peaceful protests?"

"You're being cautious," she said. "By way of explanation, our grandson has just written an A+ essay on the food riots and demonstrations in Haiti."

"That's a good cause," Albert said. "Good for him."

"How old is your grandson?" Hilda asked.

"Tim is thirteen."

"Lucky you. Our grandchildren are preschoolers. Sometimes I wish we'd had our children earlier, too, so we wouldn't be grandparents in our senior years. It makes everything harder."

Shirley did not like where Hilda's talk was taking the conversation. "All our grandchildren are very lucky. They're not going hungry."

"Our son works for Oxfam."

That sealed it. Shirley decided on the spot she did not like Hilda. Suddenly, Tony appeared and Albert introduced him to his wife. "I was just explaining to your wife that our son works for Oxfam. She seems very interested in global poverty."

"Really?" Tony turned to Shirley. "Ah, that's our grandson's doing. He's awakened our consciousness."

"Isn't it wonderful what we can learn from the young? I look forward to watching ours grow up. Have you other grandchildren?"

No Shirley did not like Hilda or her family one bit. It sounded to Shirley as though Hilda Schroeder was in competition with her for whom could do the most good in the world. It didn't help that Tony was now having an intelligent conversation with the couple about Oxfam's role in sustainable agriculture. He only broke it off when they collected their tee-off time and golf clubs. Soon they found themselves outside with Ramsey and Rose who were playing with Max and his wife, Nadia. Max owned the big supermarket that was newly built on the edge of town. Shirley wanted to talk to him, too, but decided now was not the time to bring up more conversations about food supplies.

Instead Shirley started off with an innocuous request. "Let them go ahead of us," she said to her three partners. While the other foursome stepped up to the green Shirley remained chirpy. "You don't mind, do you?"

"Not at all," Albert said.

The other two men let the women go first. Tony took the opportunity to introduce Albert to Ramsey and Max. It seemed to Shirley that Tony was already behaving like a politician. He seemed serious about Christopher's suggestion that he run for council. Meanwhile Shirley ignored Hilda. She pretended to watch Rose and Nadia tee-off. She wasn't going to play the role of a politician's wife. Tony continued to talk to Albert about Ramsey and Max as they played the first hole. There was plenty to say since both of them were not only old friends, but long-standing members of the community and fellow directors on the Dellport Golf & Country Club board. By now Shirley was feeling so aggressive she pulled out her iron, placed her ball on the tee, positioned herself beside the golf ball, wiggled her legs and feet to take a proper stance, glared at the white thing that sat below her vision, and swung hard. Her eyes followed the rising ball as it cleared the length of the fairway and landed on the green where it rolled. In her eagerness she had been so hasty that Ramsey Reisch was still walking away. He turned to witness her ball roll into the hole whereupon he began to wave and shout, "A hole in one."

The others in his foursome returned to the putting green, looked down into the hole, looked up and cheered Shirley. From her distance she could see their arms waving over their heads.

"You forgot to warn me about your wife's skill," Albert said shaking his index finger at them.

Shirley stood with her arms akimbo and mouth hanging open. "I'm as surprised as you."

Tony congratulated her and said, "You know what this means, dear?"

"What?"

"A round of drinks on the house, paid by you."

"It's a tradition at most places," Albert said chuckling.

"Worth the expense," Shirley said.

After the game Shirley walked up to the bar and ordered a bottle of champagne. Rose walked over to her and gave her a hug. "Congratulations, my dear."

"Give this woman here a glass," Shirley said. They raised their flutes in a toast. The men started ordering beers. "What would you like to drink, Nadia?"

"I'll have a cold glass of white wine, please."

"And you, Hilda?"

"Oh, just a ginger ale for me. You are a player of extremes. First a hole-in-one. Then a ball in the rough under a tree."

No, Shirley really didn't like Hilda. It is impossible to keep a close circle of intimate friends and Hilda didn't belong here. She broke the circle of intimacy between Shirley and the other women who played golf here. As much as her husband might want to know them where was the time to fit them in? Turning her back on Hilda Shirley made a toast with nearly every player now crowded into the bar. Twenty teams of four were registered for the tournament. That added up to close to eighty toasts. The mood was celebratory. The bartender kept filling her glass from the champagne bottles she insisted he open although she was the only player, besides Rose, who opted for the bubbly, and Rose only had the one glass. Shirley proceeded to get drunker and drunker. She wasn't a drinker and soon she started swaying. She grew so unsteady the crowd held her up to protect her from tipping onto the floor.

Albert and Hilda left early thanking Tony for an unforgettable round of golf. After the cup was given out to the winners of the tournament Tony and Ramsey helped Shirley to the car. What happened when they arrived home remained a blank but in the morning she did wake up in her own bed sober. She remembered nothing of the previous day and felt perfectly fine.

She found Tony in the kitchen deeply engrossed reading the morning paper. "Good Morning," she said to get his attention.

"Good Morning, dear," he said without raising his head.

"Must be interesting news."

Tony peered over his paper. "It's been a terrible June. The worst since the depression."

"Really?"

"I'm not exaggerating."

"I didn't think you were. I've never known you to exaggerate. That's my department."

Tony placed the open paper on the table. "We have to talk about food."

For an instant Shirley thought he was referring to the food crisis in Haiti but soon sensed that he wasn't being philosophical or ideological or altruistic. "Shall I make you some breakfast?"

"In a minute. First we have to talk. We've been eating at the club a lot this month."

"Yes, since Felicia left. Maybe Pamela's right. Maybe she's not coming back."

"Paolo has gone to join her."

"He has?"

"Yes, Max told me."

"Oh." Shirley often saw Paolo when she went shopping at the supermarket. He filled the shelves in the produce department. He'd worked for Max ever since Felicia started with them beginning at the small supermarket and now at the larger place on the edge of town. Paolo had been made a manager at the new, bigger store. He, too, was a loyal and reliable worker.

"It's not a problem. Max can hire students to do his job."

"Yes," Shirley said recognizing that Tony was thinking in terms of an employer who needed to hire a replacement to get the work done whereas she was thinking in terms of an employer who's lost a reliable servant and a mother whose daughter has lost a loyal friend.

"We've spent a lot of money at the golf club."

"We have?"

"Last night topped the record."

Shirley began to recover her memory. She laughed.

"Shirley, stocks have tumbled."

"Are we broke?"

"No, but I think we need to economize. Our investments aren't as secure as I would like them to be. These are our retirement savings. Everything is volatile. Rocketing oil prices. A weak dollar. There's likely to be more bad financial news. I can't foresee anything improving soon."

"Is it that bad?"

"Yes, investors are dumping auto stocks. It's reached the technical definition of a bear market."

"Holy moly," Shirley said. She'd overheard Tony talk to Ramsey often enough to know there were bear and bull markets and that bull was better than bear. Usually Tony didn't talk to her about their finances or investments, although he did take her along when they went to meet with their bank manager. She'd always let him make the decisions. She'd always assumed she was present simply to cosign the papers.

Looking down at the newspaper spread across the top of the table she stared at the double sheet. He had the business section opened so she couldn't read any of the fine print upside down, not that any of it would make sense to her. "Well, we can start eating more meals at home." Immediately Shirley's mind raced ahead to her birthday. "Can we still afford to celebrate my birthday?"

Tony reached over and covered the back of her hand with the palm of his. "Yes, of course, dear. We'll make it a very special occasion. Our date."

Shirley smiled. She had some ideas of where she wanted to go and what she wanted to do but now was not the time to share them. "Scrambled eggs and toast coming up," she said rising.

Later Shirley picked up the local paper that was delivered to the front porch. It was such a nice day she decided to sit outside to read it. On Monday, June 30, 2008, the front page pictured the winners of the mixed golf tournament at the Dellport Golf & Country Club. Before reading the article she tried to figure out how her foursome had not won after their great start with her hole-in-one. Surely that stroke alone would have brought down their overall score. She read that all the players of the winning foursome had played well beating her foursome by ten strokes. They didn't even place. Yet she did get a mention. "Shirley Palmer surprised everyone with her first swing off the first hole by scoring a hole-in-one. Afterwards she treated all the participants to drinks at the bar."

So much for her luck. It had cost her. Between that expense

and the plunging value of their stocks she was on the hook for home cooking.

The other picture that caught her eye showed a scene in the local courtroom. The caption above read: Pilot Off To Prison For Drug Smuggling. This man was no Dougie Nicholl. He was convicted of smuggling a quarter tonne of cocaine on his plane. Serious stuff. 'He will be back in court to set a date for sentencing.' The Justice, Julie Baxter, said she would need solid conditions to consider his release because he was a pilot and a flight risk. Shirley speculated that this must be her first case. She was recently sworn in as a magistrate. Here was news she could share with Tony and ask him who would be their lawyer now that Julie was promoted.

Opening the local newspaper Shirley started skimming the articles. There was one about New Canadians being sworn in. Shirley was surprised to read that there would be forty new citizens. She remembered there were only a dozen when Felicia and Paolo became citizens. The whole family had attended that ceremony to witness them taking their oath of citizenship. They were all so proud of the couple.

One page was devoted to local police matters and there certainly was enough happening to keep the force busy investigating crimes. On the street where Pamela lived someone had stolen a car on Saturday night. Someone else had stolen cases of beer. The police were releasing a victim's name. It made Shirley tired just reading about it.

On the back page an ad caught her attention. Dellport's Farmers' Market was opening on Wednesday afternoons as well as Saturday mornings in the municipal park behind the town hall. Immediately she decided that that's where she would go to buy fresh produce, local meat, prepared foods and baked goods for their meals at home. Never mind that shopping at the market cost more. She would be doing good.

Then Shirley started thinking about the demonstration she was planning with Tim and his school friends. The best place to hold it would be outside the supermarket. Folding the paper she went into the house to phone her grandson.

Chapter 16

Dellport Farmers' Market

The market had the atmosphere of a fair, a joyous gathering. Shirley felt uplifted as soon as she got out of her car. Everything about it was attractive: signs above all the stalls, smiling people chatting with each other, children in groups laughing together, obedient dogs on leashes, sellers busy with customers. It also helped that the weather was fine. Shirley was struck with the variety of goods on sale, not just food but craft tables. And not just goods for sale but information booths. Of course, she bumped into people she knew.

"Fancy meeting you here, Shirley."

"Good morning, Christopher. Hello, Dorothy."

"Hello Shirley. Isn't it nice they're holding the market twice a week now?"

"This is my first visit. Do you come often?"

"Yes, we were here on Saturday too. Julie's too busy to shop but we like the outing, don't we, Dorothy?"

"It gets me out of the house. It's not as crowded today as it was on Saturday. How's Maud?"

"Tony's gone to visit her," Shirley said.

"Ah, as we speak," Christopher said.

"He goes most mornings."

"Does she recognize him?"

"No, not really."

"That's what I'd heard," Dorothy said. "I would like to see her again. Maybe she'd perk up if I went? Maybe she'd remember me?"

"She might. She's remembers the past better than the present."

"I'm like that too, aren't I, Christopher?"

"You're still sharp as a tack, Dorothy."

"You should go," Shirley said with encouragement. "I find it all very depressing, but, of course, Tony is loyal."

"He's a good son. He always was. I rarely see my son anymore."

"You know he's in Hong Kong," Christopher said gently by way of explanation and excusing someone who lives so far away for not being present.

"Yes, Tony mentioned that."

"Richard James, my uncle, has moved into the retirement home."

"Has he?"

"Yes, I suppose I could visit him and take Dorothy to see Maud."

"I'll tell Tony you were asking after her," Shirley said smiling at the pair. She was thinking about passing on congratulations to Julie but they started to walk away. Then someone else approached her.

"Why, Shirley Palmer, I haven't seen you in a donkey's age."

"Hi, Len." Shirley looked him up and down. He was wearing jeans and a plaid shirt with the sleeves rolled up to his elbows. He hadn't changed his dress habits since high school.

"How's it going?"

"Well, and you?"

"Great. Been playing the banjo at the Bletch with the gang on Wednesday nights."

"You always were good in Music."

Len laughed. "You, too, Shirley. You couldn't play an instrument but you could sing."

"Well, all I sing now are hymns."

Len laughed again, more uproariously. "Say, you know Paolo comes too. Only he's gone out west to Vancouver. I'd like to go to British Columbia sometime. I hear it's nice out there."

"He went to join Felicia and their son, Patrick."

"Rumour is they plan on staying."

"Well, I don't know about that. Sometimes there's a smidgen of truth in rumours and sometimes it's all lies."

"Ain't that the truth? Well, Shirley, it's nice seeing 'ya. You look great. Life's sure been good to you."

"It has, Len. Say 'Hi' to the old gang from me."

"Will do."

Shirley stood in a reverie watching Len walk away and mingle with the crowd who were lined up at a table with information put out by the local archives. She could have ended up married to a guy like Len if she'd stayed in Dellport instead of quitting high school that fateful summer and going north to her uncle's resort to work. What would it be like married to the likes of Len? She supposed it would have been better than what her poor late mother endured. She thought she remembered hearing Len had married someone from high school, someone much younger, not anyone she knew. Most of them ended up married to their high school sweethearts. Nothing adventurous about them. Still, she supposed they were good people, in their own way. None of them attended the church on her side of town or belonged to the golf course. If they did play golf they went to the driving range. Most of them had boats and went fishing. She remembered they always had boats, aluminum ones, tagging behind their vehicles on trailers. She never liked boats and she never liked fishing. Her father flipped his when driving with her brother and they both drowned. He had been drinking. He was often drunk. It was a tragic accident that her mother never got over. At the resort Shirley shied away from boats. Monty didn't like boats any more than she did though they liked to go swimming in the lake. Shirley shook those memories out of her brain. What was happening to her that she was thinking about the past? She'd end up like Maud if she wasn't careful. They were especially bad memories so why was she thinking so lovingly about that earlier time of her life?

Pamela was a good swimmer. Shirley saw to that. She made sure her daughter had lessons and learned properly. Johnny was a good swimmer, too. In fact, he was good enough to enter competitions. His room was still full of ribbons and trophies. He also liked boats but never owned one. She wouldn't allow it. There wasn't much she denied her son but a boat was outlawed. That never stopped him from driving his friends' crafts. Suddenly Shirley had a piercing thought. Could it be that he was at her uncle's resort? What if all along that was where he'd been? Why not? Where else would he have gone? Only now had it occurred to her that her son might have done what she did.

Shirley turned on her heels and was ready to charge home when she stopped in her tracks. On second thought, she decided she needed a plan. They would go to the beach. How long had it been since they had had a picnic on the beach? Not since last year.

There were more lineups now. She found a stall halfway down the row that was full of fresh produce. Looking above at the sign that read 'Wilhelm Family Farm' Shirley approached the stall under the canopy. Could it be? "Hello Eva."

"Hello, Shirley."

Eva Moser, now Eva Wilhelm, looked like she had in high school only her blonde hair was now bleached and unnatural looking; her beautiful skin was very wrinkled, not smooth; and instead of being tall and skinny, she was now muscular. Who would have guessed she'd end up a farmer's wife? Shirley patiently waited her turn feeling guilty that she had never gotten in touch with Eva when she returned to Dellport years ago. Yet why would she? They really had nothing in common. It seemed one of the most popular stands at the market so she must be doing well.

"This must keep you busy," Shirley said nodding to the counter full of produce when it came her turn to be served.

"It's been a bountiful year." Eva crossed her arms over her chest.

"I can see that." Shirley bobbed her head up and down, her eyes moving from Eva to the produce, all stuff she'd grown.

"I haven't seen you at the market before."

"No, my first visit. Usually I buy everything at the grocery store but I thought I'd give this a try. I'm planning a picnic." She concentrated on looking over everything as if it was the most natural thing in the world for her to be in front of Eva's stall. "I'll take some cucumbers and tomatoes."

Eva pulled some bags from her cache and dumped the cucumbers then the tomatoes in the bag. She stacked the cardboard containers to reuse.

"And strawberries."

Eva left the berries in their basket container and carefully placed it inside a small bag which she tied. "So they won't roll and get bruised," she said placing the smaller bag beside the larger one.

"I'll also have some of that nice leaf lettuce."

"Is it alright if I add it to the bag with the cucumbers and tomatoes?"

"Sure. Thanks Eva. How much do I owe you?"

Eva looked inside the bag and added up the three items plus the strawberries. "Twelve dollars."

"It was good to see you and nice you're looking so well," Shirley said pulling out her wallet. She felt she was just being polite and wanted to be more honest with Eva so she added, "I'm sure I'll be back next week."

"Thanks for dropping by," Eva said.

Shirley walked the opposite row where she found a dairy farmer and bought some cheese. Then she found a baker and purchased two loaves of bread and some home-made cookies. When she got home she phoned Pamela. Tim answered. "Do you and your Mom want to go on a picnic to the beach tomorrow with me and Grandpa?"

"I'll ask Mom."

Shirley heard him calling to his mother. He returned to the phone. "Mom says that sounds good. She's finished early tomorrow. Can we meet you there at one? Lily can't come. She's working. And my Dad, of course."

"Yes, I realize that but I'm glad you and your Mom can join us. Tell her I'm bringing cheese sandwiches, and treats. Just bring your bathing suits and towels."

"And something to drink. I always get thirsty at the beach."

"Good thinking. We have blankets, chairs, and a beach umbrella. Meet us just south of the lifeguard's chair. I find it's always quieter there. Away from the snack bar."

"Thanks, Grandma. See you tomorrow."

Chapter 17

At the Beach

Overhead the gulls shrieked, their sound like squeals of painful disdain. Shirley held down her straw hat on top of her head with one hand. The picnic basket she was holding dropped into the crook of her elbow. In the other hand she carried a beach umbrella. Tony had four folded chairs under one arm and a blanket and towels under the other. A warm wind blew their loose clothing, hugging their body and limbs like a second skin. When they stopped bits of sand smacked their bare limbs and face making their skin feel like it was diseased. Struggling against the elements they finally secured the blanket with four chairs on the corners. Shirley placed the picnic basket in the middle of the blanket and Tony secured the umbrella into the sand at the edge of the blanket to cast a shadow over two chairs where they sat and stared out at the rolling waves breaking over the sand dunes.

"There they are," Tony said waving.

Shirley turned her head and watched the pair trundle over the loose sand. It did not make for easy walking. With each step their feet sank and their legs pulled awkwardly. One of the beaches further north along the lake allowed cars to park. Every morning a grader packed the sand down to make it possible for tires to travel over the sand but Shirley never liked going there. She preferred their local beach. It was smaller but natural and less crowded. They were lucky to have this bit of paradise so close to home. "Isn't this lovely," she said when Pamela and Tim plopped their bodies down on the blanket.

"It is. Thanks, Mom, for suggesting it."

"Good you're both wearing hats," Tony said. "Still sit back here in the shade."

Pamela wriggled her body to sit between the two chairs. "Why aren't you wearing a hat?"

"I forgot."

"He means he could only find his golf visor."

"Not much good for covering the top of your head," Pamela cautioned.

Tim opened the cooler. "Want a drink?" He lifted a can of pop in one hand and a lemonade in the other.

"I'll have a lemonade," Shirley said. "Hand me the basket, please, Tim."

He stood to give her the can and the blanket sank. Then he reached for the basket by falling forward onto his knees.

"I have to tell you where all this food came from," Shirley said. "I went shopping yesterday at the Dellport Farmers' Market. The bread comes from Happy Farm Bakery as do the sweets which you get after you eat your cheese sandwich. The cheese comes from Marshall's Dairy Farm on County Road Seven. And all the lovely greens come from Wilhelm's farm as do the tomatoes and strawberries which you also get for dessert."

"Grandma, that's great."

"See what an influence you've had on us, Tim. We won't tell Max."

"We might," Shirley said, winking at her grandson.

"Are you two up to something?" Pamela asked.

Tim shook his head while chewing a mouth full of bread and cheese.

Tony said something about the exorbitant cost of local goods.

Tim swallowed. "Maybe when Paolo returns you could talk to him and suggest the grocery store stock more local produce rather than shipping in stuff from California and Florida."

"Is Paolo coming back? Rumour is that he and Felicia are planning on moving west."

"I don't know. I haven't heard from her. Have you?" Shirley did not look at her daughter when asking her question.

"No. She must be having a good time."

"If you say so."

"What's that supposed to mean?"

"Now, now," Tony said. "We're here to enjoy ourselves, not to lay blame."

They chewed in silence.

Pamela squeezed her empty sandwich bag into a ball. "Before I eat anymore I'm going in for a swim."

"I guess that old rule about waiting an hour is no longer in effect."

"No, Mom. Are you coming, Tim?"

He took a swig and finished his drink. "Sure."

"I'll wait," Shirley said.

"Me, too."

Tony and Shirley watched mother and son run into the waves. Pamela splashed Tim and he swam off into the deeper water before standing up at a distance on a shallow sand dune. As soon as his mother reached him he took off again. Then a third time. After that they made their way back following the same routine. There were only three sand dunes within safe distance. They arrived back at the blanket laughing and spraying water. Tim shivered and clutched his towel around him.

"Here," Shirley said. "Have a sweet. Do you want a brownie or a date square?"

"Brownie, please."

"Date square," Pamela said. "Thanks, Mom."

"One of each," Tony said.

"Grandpa," Tim laughed. "Does that mean I can have two brownies?"

"You certainly can," Shirley said. She opened the container of strawberries. "Try some of these. They're delicious."

"Remember when we used to go to that farm in the country to pick strawberries?"

"Yes," Shirley said. "That was before Eva married Jack Wilhelm. His parents ran the farm then."

"I remember going there," Tony said. "In those days my Mom made jam. She always loved it when we brought her baskets of strawberries to preserve."

"You guys must have picked a lot," Tim said.

"We did, although I think I ate as many as I picked," Pamela admitted.

"We have pictures of you sitting between the rows of plants, your face smudged red around the mouth." Tony took a few berries and pulled off the stem with his teeth before putting the whole berry in his mouth.

"Dorothy Baxter says she wants to visit Maud."

"I'm sure Mom would like that."

"Why don't we ever visit great-grandma?"

"I don't think she'd recognize you anymore." Tony tucked his chin into his neck and looked over at Tim.

"That doesn't matter. We should still visit her."

"You're right, Tim. Just because she doesn't recognize me doesn't mean she wouldn't recognize you or would like to have us with her."

"Grandpa goes to see her most mornings," Shirley said.

"Can I come with you tomorrow?" Tim asked.

"Of course you can."

"Do you know where Johnny is?"

Everyone stopped eating and stared at Shirley.

"Why, Mom? Do you think he should come home and visit Grandma?" Pamela asked.

"Yes, and I think I know where he is."

"You do?" Tony asked.

Shirley looked directly at her daughter while answering. "I think he's at my uncle's lodge."

"How do you know? Did you call him?" Pamela asked.

"No, I just figured it out. Well, is he?"

"I'm not supposed to say." Pamela took another date square and bit into it letting the crumbs fall on her lap, her wet thighs, and on the blanket. The crumbs on her thighs stuck.

"So, I guessed right."

"Well I wouldn't have figured that out in a million years," Tony said.

"What's he doing there?" Tim asked.

"Working. What else would he be doing?"

"At least now we know he's safe."

"I wouldn't go that far," Shirley said looking over in the direction of the pier beyond which was Montgomery's Marina, a place she avoided like the plague.

"Have I met this uncle?" Tim asked. "The one who owns the lodge?"

"No, he's not really your uncle," Pamela said.

"How come? If he's my uncle's uncle then isn't he a great uncle?"

"No, I don't think it works that way," Tony said.

"If great-grandma dies we can let him know and then he'll come home for the funeral."

"Yes, Tim, we can do that," Shirley said.

"That's a bit macabre," Pamela said. "You're getting more like your sister every day."

"I think it has more to do with his age," Tony said. "He's just being realistic."

"Speaking of your sister, where is she working?"

"She isn't actually working, Mom. She's volunteering and gaining experience with therapy dogs. She's lucky she got that scholarship to pay her tuition. Not to mention the help all of us give her with her other expenses."

Pamela stretched out on the blanket and put her canvas hat over her face. Tim opened another can and asked if anyone wanted more to drink. They sat in silence watching the beach activity. Later they all went for a swim. Afterwards it was a struggle to pack up their things but they managed the task with a few giggles and some cooperative effort. Tony and Shirley said good bye to Tim and Pamela then placed towels on the seats of the car before sitting on them in their wet bathing suits. As they drove the short distance home Tony thanked his wife for arranging a fine afternoon at the beach with family. "And I can't tell you how relieved I am to know where Johnny is. How did you figure it out?"

"Female intuition."

Chapter 18

Maud

Maud stopped on her slow shuffle to the bathroom when Tony and Tim arrived at her room. "What are you doing here?"

"Good Morning, Mother. Just come for a visit with Tim."

Maud looked groggily at Tim. "Who's he?"

"You remember Tim? Your great-grandson? Pamela's son."

"No, don't remember him. What about Johnny?" She seemed to be getting shorter the longer she stood.

"He's my son. Your grandson."

" I know that. Where is he?"

"He's up north working."

"He isn't here?" Maud asked sounding forlorn.

"No, he went away to get work."

Maud turned away from Tony and Tim, and passing them, continued into the bathroom. She didn't shut the door behind her so Tony ushered Tim into the room to give Maud her privacy. It was a long room that had a bed against one wall. Beside that was a sofa, a two-seater. Tony suggested they sit there. Across from them, below the window, was a high backed chair with a footstool. The impression from Maud's backside was still imprinted on the seat. Across the bed was a dresser and on top of that a television. Tony leaned into Tim.

"That's the first time she's ever asked after Johnny. I think you remind her of him. I know you're not like him in any way, but, seeing you must have triggered a memory of him when he was your age."

"I guess so."

"What do you think? Getting old can be pretty sad."

"I guess so." Tim looked away from the window and searched the room with curious eyes.

"Not what you expected?"

"No, but I'm glad I came. I haven't seen her since Christmas."

"She's gone downhill since then." Tony dropped his chin and pondered the condition of his aging mother. He hoped beyond reason that she could stay where she was because the thought of her having to go into another facility saddened him. At least in the retirement home she knew many of the residents.

"She's taking a long time in the bathroom. Do you think she's alright?"

"Yes, we'd hear her in distress if she wasn't."

They waited in silence. Tony thought about his marrying Shirley. It was an odd thought as he rarely visited his past like this but he supposed appropriate given everything that was happening to them: his mother, his son, his step-grandchildren. All his life he had been the pride of his mother who never understood his choice for a wife. She expected he knew very little about women and she was right. At school he was a joy to all his teachers. He knew subjects of learning from them. He knew his own ideas which he needed to convey to gain good grades. He didn't know girls except for his sister, Jane, and he avoided her.

When Maud made her slow reentry, Tony asked, "Do you want to go to the atrium?"

"Is that what you want?" Maud held onto the side of the dresser and turned herself around to face the door. It was a wide, metal door, a fire door from the days when the place was a hospital. The doors had to be kept shut for fire regulations which cut the residents off from one another so Tony liked to take her into the public space. Otherwise she would sit by herself until someone came to get her for her next meal or one of her appointments. There was an on-site hairdresser and, although Maud had a standing appointment for every Thursday morning, she tended to forget what day it was and needed reminders. Tony put a calendar on the wall and kept it open to the current date but Maud rarely looked at it. The servers at breakfast talked to the residents about their day but by the time Maud got up from the table and walked away she'd forgotten what they'd said to her.

Tony held the door wide and indicated to Tim where they were going.

Tim held the second door open wide that led into the atrium. Maud shuffled through while mumbling to him, "Most people here need walkers. Not me. I don't use a walker or a cane."

"That's great, Great-Grandma." Tim knew he sounded silly, even patronizing, but she was being a bit that way too. She was very short. He thought she must have shrunk.

"Well who's this fine fellow? Is this Tim?"

"Yes," Tony said staying behind his mother but catching the eye of the elderly gentleman in front of her. "Tim meet Richard James."

"Hello." Tim stopped and stared at a very thin man. He had a walker that was extended to its full height.

"I know your grandpa from town," he said. "Me and your great grandma used to play golf together, didn't we Maud?"

Maud looked up at him. "Did we?"

"We sure did. We had some great times together. I often see your Mom here."

"Yes. It's her job," Tim said. "I mean, she comes to visit great grandma, too, but she also has clients she has to visit who live here."

"I know. She's a good lady. We all love her here." Richard turned to Tony. "Christopher tells me Shirley got a hole-in-one?"

"She did. First time ever."

"First time for everything," Richard said. "She'll be remembered for that. Are you going to stay for the music?"

"We'll stay for awhile," Tony said. He led them to some seats that were set up in front of a piano. "You don't mind, do you, Tim?" he quietly asked.

"No," Tim said looking around the room. He was the youngest one in the audience. He guessed the two teenage girls behind the small canteen were volunteers. He sat beside his grandpa. The woman who was going to play the piano for them explained that she taught music at a high school in another town and that she was here visiting her mother. Tim wondered if maybe he should volunteer to play sometime. It would be good practice and it would give him some volunteer hours which he needed next year as part of his community service. When intermission came Tony turned to his mother, "We have to go now, but you stay in the atrium with Richard so you can listen to the music."

Maud nodded she would. As they departed Tim noticed the two girls were serving juice to the residents. "I think I'd like to volunteer here," he said.

"That's a fine idea."

"Maybe I could play for them."

"You could offer. Do you want to drop into the office now?"

"Maybe I'll talk to my Mom about it first."

Outside the humidity was building. "It's going to be a scorcher," Tony said.

Tim did not mention on the ride home that he was making plans with his Grandma to hold a demonstration. He'd given her his word. "No need to scare anyone," she'd said. Only now he felt he was being disloyal to his Grandpa and his Mom. Tim felt like he had to pretend to be somebody else in front of them. Yet they were family and always supportive and helpful. They took him seriously. Not all adults took teenagers seriously. Sometimes teenagers didn't take each other seriously. Mostly they taunted one another. Tim tried not to do that too much, except with his sister.

Besides, why would holding a demonstration scare people? Grandma said he had to talk to his friends in secret, too. None of them were taking the demonstration frivolously, not because of the secrecy, but because of the subject. There was nothing shameful about being associated with such a noble cause, yet now Tim felt he was covering up something embarrassing. He pretended to take a short nap on the drive home in case he betrayed their plans.

Chapter 19

A Demonstration

The following Friday, July 11, Linda got into Shirley's car and, after thanking her for the ride, explained that she was the only one coming.

"Have Barbara and Jane chickened out?"

"Yes, they said they have to remain loyal to Max."

"They couldn't tell me that."

"They knew you'd put up an argument."

"They know me well and I know them well. They're not being loyal to Max. They're being loyal to their bank book. They always were selfish."

"They're like most people, Shirley. They like to save money when buying food."

"They like to save money when shopping, period."

"A paradox."

"Pardon?"

"It's a paradox," Linda explained. She repeated Shirley's line. "They like to save money when shopping. A paradox is a contradiction. You can't go shopping without spending money."

"Linda, you always were smart in English class."

"Life is full of paradoxes. Like the Virgin Birth."

Shirley hooted and slapped the steering wheel with the open

palm of her hand. "That's a good one. I've never believed that one."

Linda's voice was upbeat with her banter but she became serious. "Me neither, but my mother did."

"Mine, too. She didn't believe me when I told her that I didn't do anything to get pregnant with Pamela. In her day it didn't occur to her to say what I could have done not to get pregnant."

"No," Linda sighed. "We didn't do anything. That's the trouble. No one gave us any advice. We let the men do it all. We let them take the lead. We didn't have anything to do with it."

"Ah, Linda. You sound so sad. Do you think we missed out on something?"

"I do."

"See," Shirley said holding her gaze steady, not on the road, but on her thoughts that she wanted to put into words. She gripped the steering wheel to prevent her hands from flying off before she could get her words out of her mouth. "This is the thing with what you were saying about a, whatever."

"Paradox?'

"Yeah, it might not be a paradox. It could be that we had virgin births because we had virgin sex. Do you get my drift?"

"Yes, unfortunately I do, Shirley."

"Well, here we are." Shirley parked her car on the street in front of the house.

"Does Pamela approve of this?"

"She doesn't know. She's at work. So is Clinton and so is Lily. Only Tim is home."

Shirley opened the door without knocking. "Yoo-hoo. Anybody home?"

"We're in the kitchen, Grandma."

Shirley and Linda walked down the hall into the kitchen. Tim was there with two friends. "Hi," Shirley said extending her hand. "I'm Shirley Palmer, Tim's maternal grandmother. And this here is Linda Leach."

"Yes, we know who you are. You're Rupert's grandmother."

"Yes," Linda said. "This year's valedictorian." Linda beamed at the boys unashamed about her feelings of joy for her only grandson. "And you are?"

"I'm Tyler."

"I'm Ryan."

"Are you related?" Linda asked.

The boys laughed. "Yes, we're twins."

"Well that explains why you look and sound alike," Shirley said. "I see you've got all the materials we need." She walked over to the table and started lifting items to inspect.

"Ryan and Tyler's dad took over the hardware store," Tim said.

"Oh, of course," Shirley said. "Tony said he had twins."

"They got us these stakes and bristol board."

"That's great, boys. Of course I've met your dad." Shirley turned and stood close to them. "Are we it?"

"We are. Everyone else is either away on holiday or busy but we got lots of support."

Shirley nodded. There was no point in reminding her grandson that support meant being present to take up the fight. Boots on the ground, so to speak. Still, they were a respectable number and they went to work making signs.

The five signs they made fit into the trunk and the three boys fit into the back seat. They headed to the supermarket that was on the outskirts of town. Both ends of town were built up. To the south was the new police station and light industrial buildings. To the north was a shopping mall and box stores. Shirley chose to park near the entrance away from where most cars were parked. She felt a tinge of excitement popping the trunk knowing that this was the moment. Her sign simply said 'Buy Local'. She'd chosen to use a green marker against the white board. She'd chosen a simple cursive font, one word on the top with the second word below it. She'd made the letters large and coloured them thickly so the words stood out and were easy to read from a distance.

Linda wrote her sign in a calligraphy style which looked more like the style of script used for a wedding invitation than a protest sign. It didn't help that she'd chosen to use a pink marker. In response to the criticism leveled at her from the twins she'd outlined the words in black marker which made the design look like an ad for sexy underwear. Since her sign was only getting worse with their suggestions and interference, the others chose to keep quiet. Her sign read: 'Where does your food grow?' It was hard to read unless you stood directly in front of the board. Still, she was pleased as punch with it and proudly carried it with the word side against the front of her body so it couldn't be read until she was at the store and in position.

Tim's reflected his message from his essay. He'd written 'GLOBAL FOOD SHORTAGES' in thick and heavy upper case letters and used a brown marker. Tyler and Ryan had read Tim's essay and in class heard him speak about the food riots so they, too, made political statements. Tyler's sign read: 'Feed The World'. He'd used a sketchy script and black marker. Ryan's read: 'Food Prices?' His was the only sign with punctuation and, since the black and brown markers were being used by his friend and brother, he wrote his message in bright red.

When they reached the front of the store Shirley regretted they hadn't brought a drum or tambourine, something to bang or make a noise. "Never mind," Tim said. "We have a chant." With that he and the twins started to shout, "Fair, fair, fair. Let's be fair. Fair, fair, fair. Let's be fair."

Lifting her sign up and down to the rhythm of the chant, Shirley joined them. The boys walked in a tight circle. They were positioned between the rows of shopping carts and the automatic doors. They were careful not to step on the rubber pad that opened the doors and that the shoppers were using to enter and exit. Linda stood directly in front of the store window waving her sign silently. Shirley decided to break from the boys and greet the shoppers. When she spoke to anyone who hesitated to enter she asked, "Do you know where your food is grown?" If they stuck with her after the first question she continued and asked, "Are you paying a fair price to farmers?" "What about the starving and the poor?" Those who got the full complement of questions were few in number.

The protesters were in the shade from the building that faced west. Linda watched the shoppers who hurried across the parking lot to reach the store doors. Many rushed past Shirley and the demonstrators. Some stopped long enough to take a good look at the five protesters and read their signs. A few challenged Shirley. Was she a farmer? Was she on a budget? Where did she shop?

Within less than half an hour Max appeared. "Shirley, what are you doing?"

"We're demonstrating."

Max walked in front of his store and looked at the motley crew. He watched his shoppers enter his store and appraised the situation before going back inside.

Within minutes they heard sirens. Nonplussed they continued with their demonstration. After all, sirens rang out continually, especially in the summer with tourists travelling to the region. Even when two police cars veered into the mall the five protesters continued. Shirley was surprised when the patrol cars stopped in front of them. She thought maybe someone had fainted inside the store and soon an ambulance would arrive. When one of the officers approached her and asked her for a permit she told him she didn't need one. She and her friend and her grandson and his friends were holding a peaceful demonstration.

"I'm afraid I'm going to have to ask you to move along," he said.

"We will not."

The officer grabbed Shirley under her elbow. She raised her arm to avoid his grasp. As he reached up Shirley knocked him over the head with her sign.

Chapter 20

At The Police Station

Unlike Clinton, Shirley was not put in a holding cell. Instead she was locked inside Albert Schroeder's office. This was not a windowless room, but neither was it a room with a view. A blind covered the small window which Shirley guessed was permanently closed, probably to keep daylight out so the computer screen could function optimally. She was not told anything and she did not ask any questions. The arresting officer, Barry Nickel, had taken her sign and firmly led her to the patrol car. She'd yelled at her grandson to call his grandfather before she was driven away. Inside the vehicle everyone was silent. At the station they were met by Albert who'd asked why Shirley was under arrest and, when told, said he would take her into his custody.

Unlike Tony who had sat calmly in this same chair, Shirley was not feeling particularly calm in the police chief's office. Unlike her husband she did not notice the large picture of the man's extended family on the desk. She did not look at the smaller picture of him and his wife. She did not see his academic diplomas on the wall between the windows. She was not familiar with his office or the new police station. She had never been inside it and neither had she been inside the old one. She was sitting as still as a statue not feeling embarrassed or shameful. What Shirley felt was totally indignant and insulted that she was being detained. They all knew who she was, but they were behaving as if they didn't. Did they really think she was some sort of criminal? Were they all stupid? Didn't they know she had been demonstrating peacefully?

All these questions and more rattled her brain. The touchstone she returned to through all the conflicting questions that raced through her mind was the picture of her dear grandson leaning into the cruiser telling her he would call Grandpa. So where was Tony? Was he at the police station? Was he talking to Albert? Was he talking to a lawyer?

Maybe she should write everything down? Yes, that would be a good idea. While everything was fresh in her mind she would write her side of the story. Only it wasn't a story, was it? It was her experience. It was what really happened.

Now she did look at the desk and there, directly in front of her, was a large pad of paper and a container full of pens. To the right was a computer screen. This was a modern facility but Albert Schroeder was her contemporary (well, maybe a few years younger, in his fifties, not sixties) and as a mature adult he still relied on pen and paper.

Shirley rooted through the cup of pens and found a Paper Mate Profile. It was the perfect tool, a nice rubber grip on the end, a quick release on top that revealed a nib with blue flowing ink. She began:

First, you have to understand my motive. My dear grandson, Tim Croft,

Holding the perfect pen above the pad of paper Shirley hesitated. What did she smell? Not the Paper Mate. No, she smelled the magic markers from the morning when she was with

Tim and his friends preparing posters and placards for the demonstration. The markers had a sharp smell that was accompanied by the frenzy of purposeful activity. That smell reminded her that earlier in the day they had worked together on what could be described as a calling. She could feel her grandson there, beside her in the office still chanting, though she knew he wasn't. Shirley had had recent bouts of smelling scents that were not actually in the air at the moment when she smelled them. Her memory had been playing tricks on her just as it was doing now. Maybe it was the excitement of doing something unusual. Maybe she couldn't contain her emotions or her senses let alone her thoughts. This made her more nervous than being detained by a police officer. She couldn't let the past catch up to her. She had to concentrate on what she needed to do.

Again she put pen to paper: "is not to blame but he is the sole inspiration behind our peaceful protest that may be considered by some to be an act of civil disobedience but was not planned as a violent confrontation. It was planned out of our caring for others who are less fortunate than ourselves and do not have enough to eat while we have so much we waste food. My grandson wrote an essay that you should all read. We should hold civic lessons at the town hall. We can do that and maybe now that we have attracted attention to our cause the citizens of Dellport will come to hear how apathetic we have been about food and local food production and how our actions have impacted food distribution to other countries who also need to return to small market farming. Let's be fair. That's all we're asking. Please give my grandson a voice. Listen to him like I have. Think of all your grandchildren and their future."

Her writing left her completely unsatisfied. It was so small — just a few scratches on a big piece of paper. It was tiny compared to what was in her head. There was so much in her head that was not written down on the piece of paper. Had she written about Oxfam? Had she described Haiti? Where was the history? Tim had won a history prize and she had not described the history that led up to their taking action. All that thinking and experience and relevance gone, omitted in her retelling, only to be replaced by some old woman's pleadings. That's how they would see her, as some old woman who has temporarily lost her senses. Well, she'd show them. She was made of sterner stuff.

Chapter 21

Community Service

Meanwhile Tony was working behind the scenes at the station to have Shirley released. He had Brenda Bain with him. He wasn't sure how it happened that she came to be his legal counsel but there she was joining him at the station. It was as if everyone in town knew immediately what was going on. He said, "I don't want this incident to become high-profile, the stuff of front page news and editorial comment."

"I understand." She didn't think he would be granted his wish but saw no point in explaining her reasons to her client. Christopher James had phoned her and she reckoned these men would pay her handsomely but she could hardly control the press.

Of course the police wanted to throw the book at Shirley. As far as they were concerned she was no different than anyone else who assaulted someone in uniform. They demanded justice when speaking to Brenda. There were grumblings throughout the station. They demanded a conviction when speaking to the chief. Why wasn't this dangerous woman behind bars? As she was taken away by her husband and lawyer there were outright comments, loud enough to be within earshot. "Ignore them," Tony said to Shirley as he led her to the car. In the car he said, "Shirley, you were breaking the law, you know?"

"How? It was a peaceful demonstration."

"It was on private property and you didn't have a permit."

"That's a small technicality."

Tony bit his tongue. He'd never been quiet with Johnny as he'd felt the responsibility of being a parent, but now he felt like a parent to a grown woman, his own wife. Why did he always end up feeling like he'd been too indulgent with the ones he loved?

Despite all their best efforts the outcome was printed in the local paper the following week:

Demonstrator sentenced to community service

Dellport – An immediate sentencing in the case of the elderly demonstrator, Shirley Palmer, was announced yesterday. The question of taking the case to court was dismissed by Brenda Bain, Mrs. Palmer's lawyer, as unnecessary given the cooperation of the guilty party and the willingness of the police to deal swiftly with the culprit. "Everything can be dealt with out of court," the lawyer told reporters.

Shirley Palmer is a local woman and grandmother to one of the demonstrators. None of the young demonstrators can be named because they are underage. Some of the parents of these minors were in court and spoke of a profound sense of betrayal that was devastating to them. They also felt that the culprit had caused mischief to the public.

The demonstration happened last Friday morning in front of Dellport Supermarket on Highway #2, owned by Max Hanover. The police were called by the owner when Shirley Palmer and the other demonstrators refused to leave after being asked by him to vacate the premises. "They were blocking the entrance and obstructing the customers who were there to shop and who wanted to get shopping carts to go inside the store."

Setting out the reason behind the punishment the lawyer

pointed out that at the age of 60 this was a first offense and not likely to be repeated. Shirley Palmer will have no criminal record.

The terms of the order dictate 75 hours of community service at the local food bank. Asked if she had anything to say Shirley murmured that she was happy to volunteer at the food bank. The owner of the food market said he is happy to have Shirley return as a loyal paying customer. Mr. Hanover also said that he donates food to the food bank.

Oblivious to all that was going on behind the scenes to arrange the expedited sentence Shirley took up the challenge of volunteering with the local food bank with her familiar enthusiasm. She told Cal, the manager, "I'm so happy to get out of the house and be of some use to others."

Cal became the ears to her talk about hunger and famine on an international scale and farmers and crops at the local level. She told him all about her grandson and his award-winning essay. She wasn't just bragging. She was informing, enlightening, sharing. She then accepted his compliments. "He must be a bright boy."

"Oh he is. Not like me. I never did too well in school, especially high school." She kept up the chatter before he could make guesses about Tim. She didn't want to have to explain too much since Cal was a recent arrival in Dellport. He didn't know all the gossip and slander and history of local families. Shirley didn't ask him where he was from or why he'd come to Dellport. It was enough to know that he was a giving person. He looked somewhat weathered, as if he'd lived rough for awhile, and he was very thin so maybe he was atoning for his sins by dedicating himself to feeding the poor. He knew them, the poor who arrived at the counter for food handouts. Cal was friendly, greeting each and every one by name and asking after their families. Cal remembered from their previous visits what food they liked and wanted. He introduced Shirley. "She's our newest recruit."

"Hi." A young woman handed Shirley her coupons.

Cal showed her how to take them.

After the young woman left Shirley said, "I'm surprised how organized your system is for handing out donations." A family entered and Cal stepped aside to let Shirley serve them.

After they'd gone with their loaded boxes she listened attentively to Cal's descriptions of their circumstances. When a middle aged couple entered, Shirley recognized them as people she knew from around town but she didn't act surprised or make judgmental comments. She took her cue from Cal and simply asked, "How old are your grandchildren now?"

"They're two, four and six."

"Wow," Shirley blurted out, but said no more.

When another couple came whom she recognized Shirley asked, "Are your parents well?" She didn't make any speculation about where they were living but when they'd gone she asked Cal.

"I don't know. For all I know they could have lost their house or apartment. Most of them who come here have lost their jobs. That's what brings them to the food bank, no income or not enough to see them through to the end of the month; that, or living on compensation because of hardship brought on by accidents or long-term illnesses."

After her first day volunteering Shirley arrived home grateful. She'd had an earful over the weekend from her daughter about plying the young with ideas of insurrection. As usual, Pamela exaggerated. "It's because of you," she'd said, "that my husband was arrested and my son nearly arrested. How can I hold up my head in this town anymore without feeling shame? I'm going to die of embarrassment. You've gone too far, as usual. I'm at my wit's end."

At that point, Shirley was reminded of the histrionics of her own mother when she thought Shirley had carried things too far. 'I'm at my wit's end!' was a familiar refrain. "Sweetie," Shirley began.

"Don't 'sweetie' me."

Shirley was left standing alone with her own confused thoughts. Mostly her mother filled her head with promise, telling her how wonderful she was and what a bright future lay ahead for a girl like her who was lively and had so many friends. It was her mother's way of making her daughter feel secure so it seemed natural for Shirley to spout opinions on things she knew nothing about and to think that her opinions mattered. As a sixty year old woman Shirley retained enough casual confidence that she dismissed Pamela with the ease of someone who has never done anything wrong.

Clinton and Lily were less harsh. In fact, they seemed a little proud of her and Tim for drawing attention to the dire situation. Yet when Shirley left Pamela's house and Clinton was alone with his wife he offered his uncensored opinion. "After Lily's gone we're going to have to keep a close eye on the relationship between our son and his grandmother."

"I know. How am I to trust her?"

"We can't. She'll turn Tim into another Johnny."

"What's that supposed to mean?"

"You know. He'll think he can do whatever he likes. Your mother doesn't have good judgement. She thinks Johnny's so innocent."

"Johnny's no different from other men."

"Oh yes he is."

"I'm not listening to this," Pamela said walking away.

Everyone else who'd been involved in the demonstration fell by the wayside mostly grateful that they had not attracted any attention to themselves. Ryan and his twin brother, Tyler, kept silent. They did not want to be interviewed by the police or the press. A different kind of gratitude from what Shirley experienced pervaded the mind of Linda Leach who didn't even phone. Shirley was so preoccupied with her own domestic circumstances she didn't call her friend either to find out how she was doing after the ordeal. In fact, Shirley didn't give Linda a second thought. In her mind it was as if those three hadn't been part of the demonstration.

Chapter 22

People Will Talk

At the supermarket customers came up to Max. People crave connection especially when it's about something that involves someone's misfortune who seems to have undeserved fortunes on her side and when it's about another's act of heroism when that other is a hard working ordinary person. "We're still your loyal customers, Max."

Many declared their allegiance to his store and business. He was hailed as a good citizen and a generous supporter of the community. Max was mindful not to get too involved in these personal conversations since he and his wife had an entire summer ahead of them playing golf with couples like Tony and Shirley Palmer. When he admitted to one loyal customer he regretted having to call the cops, Max was told that he had done the right thing and, furthermore, more people should phone them when there's trouble. "Some people let things go too far and then things get out-of-hand," one said.

"Mmm," Max said noncommittally.

"And then the police have bigger problems."

Max didn't say but he wondered if he should inform Paolo who was still on holidays. It wouldn't be fair to him to have him return to all the rumours and not know what had actually happened. Yet Max felt he couldn't start inquiring how to contact him out west as it wasn't an emergency. He was an employee, not family. He had taken an extended vacation and would be gone for most of the summer. Max could just write Paolo a letter and have him find it on his return unless his mail was being forwarded. How would Max know? He couldn't ask at the post office. He doubted that was information they could share with the public. He did know where Paolo lived but Max didn't know any of the neighbours. What was he to do? Stake out the place? See for himself?

At home Max spoke to his wife. "They should have put her behind bars," Nadia said.

"That's not the question I'm asking you now."

"Well, Max, I still think it was a mistake giving her a free pass. What better place to do penitence than behind bars?"

"Yes, repentance is a solitary task," Max said, recognizing he had to give Nadia her say before he could get an answer to his question or her support for his situation.

"At the hairdresser's," Nadia began, "Brandy told me about the twins, Tyler and Ryan. You know, the boys whose father bought the hardware store from Tony Palmer."

Max stopped listening. He knew his wife went to the same hair salon as Shirley and he knew Nadia gossiped with her hairdresser while sitting in the chair. He was in the habit of tuning her out when she told him what was said there. Max simply stopped listening. He found her gossip disagreeable and never understood why it fascinated Nadia. She was totally responsive to rumours of who said what or who was doing what as if it all mattered when all that really mattered was how dis-agreeable it was. Why couldn't she see that? Why couldn't she be more friendly? Maybe he should compliment her on her hairdo? Would that be wise or would she see it as a ruse?

Moments later Nadia asked, "So what was Tim thinking? He's supposed to be a bright boy who got good grades for writing a smart essay yet he let himself get caught up in a demonstration with his grandmother who has never taken a stand on anything, least of all where her food comes from. That woman always was too lazy to clean house or even cook. Tim's brain doesn't come from Tony since there's no genetic connection. He must have some of his father in him."

"Clinton's alright and Anthony Palmer's a good man," Max said, hoping that concluded her diversion. He thought of starting a discussion on nature versus nurture but that would lead him even further from his goal.

"So are Ryan and Tyler."

"How did Brandy know they were involved along with Tim?"

"That's what I'm saying. You didn't mention them as if by keeping silent you could spare them but everybody knows. And her friend Linda Leach. The one whose car they drove in the prom parade. You saw her outside the store, didn't you?"

"Yes, but Shirley is the only one who assaulted a police officer." Now Max felt like he was being interrogated. How the tables had turned. He felt like he was the victim by putting up a defense but he was hoping they could wrap this up before dinner was served or else he'd get indigestion while eating.

"Oh, by the way, there's a letter for you with a return address from Vancouver."

"There is?" Max never received personal mail. Grateful for the excuse to drop the topic of their unpleasant conversation, Max rushed away. He went to the front door where the mail sat on top of the entrance table. Leafing through the pile he found the letter and immediately opened it. He read:

Max, I sorry to ask but my son and wife want me to say here all summer and maybe longer. Is okay with you? I know you have many students helping in store. If okay you don't write just if not okay.

Paolo

So that settled the question of contacting Paolo. With the note in hand Max returned to the kitchen to tell Nadia who was dishing food on to two plates that the letter from Vancouver was from Paolo and he was not returning until the end of the summer, if then.

"Good for him. Those two deserve a nice long holiday."

Max sat. "Do you think it will be a problem delivering food to the food bank with Shirley helping out there?"

Setting his portion on the place mat Nadia looked at her husband with surprise. "Why should it be?"

"Oh, no reason," he said. Yet he could think of a dozen.

At the hair salon Brandy, the stylist, told her last customer what she'd told Nadia and every client who'd come in that day which was that Tim Croft and the twins, Ryan and Tyler, were demonstrating outside the supermarket with Shirley Palmer and Linda Leach. Those who hadn't heard showed surprise unless they also knew about Tim's academic honour. If they did know about the essay they thought the boy was being reckless letting himself be influenced by his grandmother instead of sticking to his grandfather as a role model. The old timers knew that school had defeated Shirley Montgomery; whereas Tony Palmer was a dedicated student who had discipline, not a scholar like Judge Baxter, but one willing to make sacrifices. By the time Brandy closed shop she was so well acquainted with the stories she considered the characters her own. Everyone involved, either directly or indirectly, was as familiar to her as her cousin, the cop who'd arrested Shirley Palmer.

Before midnight on Wednesday, July 16, 2008, Len was the last member of the banjo group to leave The Bletch. When he got home his wife, Brandy, was still awake reading a magazine in bed. It was destined to be one of a selection of magazines to replace the stale-dated ones at the salon. She liked to be the first to turn its pages then she would know what to talk about with her customers if there wasn't any gripping gossip to share. The couple had already had a long conversation about Barry Nickel who was her cousin twice removed. They'd agreed he was the kindest soul on earth. His size belied his quiet, shy, demeanor. They'd agreed he wasn't the problem. Now Len interrupted his wife's casual reading by saying that everyone at The Bletch had been talking about Shirley Palmer and noted that she had been the topic of conversation only two weeks earlier.

"Some people hog all the attention," Brandy said.

"You got it doll."

Brandy was as perfect and petite as a doll, a 'Singin' In the Rain' Debbie Reynolds kinda doll woman. Even while sitting up in bed her hair was always coloured and coiffed, her nails painted and manicured, her attire new and fashionable, her face moisturized, her eyes sparkling and her breath fresh.

"You should join us next week, Brandy."

"I just might," she said closing the pages of her magazine before turning out the light and rolling over to her husband's side of the bed.

Chapter 23

Stars Above

Tony greeted members at the Dellport Golf Club with a nod and they nodded in return. He felt grateful for that simple gesture, treating it as an indication that he was still an accepted member of the club. Lately he wondered if Pamela's hysteria would prove true and everyone in town would shun them. He'd never had reason to feel shame, but he supposed she did. Earlier in the week when he visited his mother at the retirement home Maud kept repeating, "Stars above". It was a saying he hadn't heard her evoke in years but he remembered it well enough from his youth. What did it mean, 'Stars above'? Was she avoiding cursing? Was she just making her feelings known without resorting to actually saying what she felt? Did she remember the stars above as a last hold on the outside world? Tony had never felt unhinged but if Shirley continued in this vein he might. How much could a person take?

Everyone at the retirement home had a version of events to tell. "Holy Moly," Richard had said leaning across Maud to address him. "Isn't Shirley overdoing it by demonstrating against food?"

Tony had wanted to clarify, but before he could speak, everyone sitting in the room had stared at him. He'd felt their owl-eyed heads pivoting from their wrinkled necks watching them. He'd hesitated just long enough for Maud to interject, "Whose side is she on anyway?" He could hear his mother's bones cracking.

"What made her think she'd be any good at that?"

Now at the golf club Tony could still picture himself turning from Maud to Richard forming an answer in his head to their aged prejudice about the fault with women of his wife's background but, deciding to keep silent, he'd reminded himself that he didn't have to explain her conduct to them, not that they would have understood. Indeed, if they had, would they have taken offense? He was left standing in a sea of judgments and pat phrases like "for heaven's sakes, small mercies, why on earth, knew perfectly well, really Tony." Because really indeed. For heaven's sakes it was what it was, a peaceful demonstration. Couldn't they be thankful for small mercies that no charges were laid? Why on earth indeed. Did they think the cost of food wasn't an issue? They knew perfectly well what it cost to remain fed and sheltered in the retirement home. That was a constant topic of conversation with them. Some of them were of the opinion that they were being totally ripped off, that the owners of the retirement residence were out to swindle them of their savings.

Usually Tony wasn't open to reflection or given to heady insights. Yet now he was in some emotional turmoil. He should feel pleased with himself for dealing with the problems of his family in such timely fashion. Yes, he was pleased. He hoped he wasn't simply feeling smug. That would not do. That wouldn't get him into anyone's good books. He knew he could not stand for elections. That would not happen. It was too much to ask of everyone.

During their round of golf no one alluded to the situation. Good men, each and every one of them, Tony thought. They knew when to keep quiet about personal business though Shirley seemed to agree with their grandson who was taking the approach that food was everyone's business and not a personal matter. As far as Tony was concerned it was best to draw the line. What his grandson did was write a top-notch essay. That should have been the end of the story. Congratulate the kid. Show him support but crossing the line was only asking for trouble and getting involved by demonstrating only divided people. Best to be involved in a quiet way. He would have to talk to Tim about making a donation on his behalf.

Tony kept his eye on the ball and made an easy putt confident of the course ahead.

When he got home that confidence was again tested. Shirley showed him the food she received from the food bank. She had cans that no users of the food bank wanted and fresh produce that wouldn't last overnight. "So I thought it best not to let the stuff go to waste and when I said it could be our dinner Cal agreed wholeheartedly."

"Are you sure we should be eating this?" he asked. "Where does it come from?"

"Max and Nadia delivered the produce this week and the cans have been sitting on the shelf all month."

"Does Cal take stuff home from the food bank?"

"Yes, we both did. He took some eggs and milk because we're getting a fresh delivery tomorrow. Don't fuss so," Shirley said.

"Well it seems highly irregular."

"Why?"

Tony sat down at the kitchen table. Before thinking how to answer he thought to ask, "How were Max and Nadia?"

"They seemed well."

"Friendly?"

"What do you mean?"

"Well, did they say hello?"

"Of course they said hello. They're always friendly. You mean to me or to Cal?"

"They said hello to you?"

"They're our friends."

"Well he did call the cops on you."

"Oh, for heaven's sakes, Tony. That was just a little misunderstanding."

There it was again, for heaven's sakes. It seemed to Tony that Shirley didn't fully understand the repercussions of her behaviour. While picking at his dinner provided by the local food bank, Tony mulled over that problem. Maybe he was too quick to get her released from jail? Maybe sparing Shirley the consequences of her actions left her too innocent? Maybe he was cheating her or cheating the cops?

"Do you think Cal is doing a good job at the food bank?"

"He is. I suggested that Tim could be of help, too. What do you think?"

"Well, maybe when they come back from holiday," Tony said.

"Are they going camping again?" Shirley asked.

"I think they might be renting a cottage or going to some resort up north."

"Pamela isn't talking to me. I'll ask Tim."

"Let me ask him. I want to talk to him anyway about another matter."

"What's that?"

"About making a monetary donation to the food bank in his name in recognition of his academic achievement."

"That's a marvelous idea," Shirley said stirring the salad on her plate to distribute the dressing more evenly over the colourful leaves. "What do you think is in this salad?"

"Darned if I know. Must be imported if it came in that plastic container," Tony said lifting a ribbed red leaf with the prong of his fork.

"Yes, shipped from the States. Maybe we shouldn't be eating this."

"I don't see why not if it's being sold in the supermarket."

"But that's just the point. We buy and eat this stuff without knowing where it comes from. I'll ask Max and Nadia the next time they make a delivery."

"Are you sure that's wise?"

Shirley sat up in her chair with her back rigid. "Tony, no one's ever accused me of being wise."

Tony laughed at his wife rearranging his worries. The next morning he made an appointment to talk to the bank manager who was a young woman new to the position. He'd learned she'd been transferred from an out-of-town branch. It seemed more and more that was what public and commercial institutions were doing, introducing unfamiliar faces. She was married to the new minister at their church, Reverend Brathwaite. Usually Shirley came with him but she was getting confused and growing impatient with all the insecurities around the market so finally he said he would go on his own.

Nia Brathwaite was small with a pug nose. Her skin was smooth and the colour of cocoa. Tony extended his hand to her and smiled feeling astonished by her firm shake.

When they were settled with all the papers in front of them and her screen open, Nia said, "I'd advise you against moving your funds. I know many people are panicked by the uncertainty of their investments." Nia continued asking lots of questions about his grandson while she filled out the forms. She was very adept with the computer and he complimented her on her performance. Glancing away from the screen she smiled at him then asked, "Do many people here use the food bank?"

"Yes," Tony said. "My wife volunteers there and is constantly surprised by who comes through the door. She and Tim are going together to deliver the donation."

"Are they? That's nice, leading by example."

Tony left with a large cheque in hand feeling pleased with the rearrangement of his finances. He would keep an eye on the current market. If he had to visit the bank manager again he felt confident she would oblige him.

Chapter 24

Telling Lies

Tim was confused by his mother's packing instructions. This year, instead of camping, they were going to stay at a resort but it had very basic accommodations so he would still need his sleeping bag and warm clothes for around the fire pit in the evenings. He would also need swimming trunks, shorts, lots of t-shirts and different shoes for the boat. "What boat?" he'd asked.

"Uncle Johnny's boat. He's taking us out in his boat but don't tell your grandmother."

"Why not?"

"She doesn't know we're going to see him."

"She doesn't?" Tim blinked and thought hard about what his mother was saying. "Are you sure she won't guess?"

"Yes. I know she guessed right about his whereabouts, but don't tell her we're going to her uncle's lodge. I don't want her blowing a gasket."

Tim wondered if his mother even knew her own mother. If anyone was to blow a gasket it would be her, not his grandmother. "Why doesn't she want us to visit her uncle?"

"Tim you ask a lot of questions."

"Does Grandma visit her uncle?"

"She did, a long time ago, but not since her mother died."

"Was her uncle her mother's brother?"

"Yes, I'm sorry we weren't close to these relatives but Uncle Johnny has visited your Great Uncle Charlie and he wants us to meet him."

"What do you mean? I thought he was living up north?"

Pamela huffed in exasperation.

"If I ask Dad will he tell me?"

"He'll say Grandma thinks her uncle is a bad man."

"Like she thinks Uncle Johnny is bad?"

"No. She doesn't think Johnny's bad. She just thinks he needs to be better behaved."

"Well if I can't mention where we're going then what will I say to her?" He knew his grandmother would figure things out because she pried until she knew what she wasn't supposed to know. Why were they treating his grandmother like a 3 year old who cannot be told things?

"You'll think of something," Pamela said leaving him to pack his own things in a large duffel bag that was made from green canvas and actually had wheels at one end so he didn't have to carry it over his shoulder. He could simply pull it. His mother had purchased one for Lily, too, but hers was blue so they could tell them apart. Lily thought she would have to stay with her grandparents and miss their family holiday because she had to stick to her commitment to volunteer and try to find work that paid to save money for university but her parents said this holiday was too important to miss. They couldn't tell their grandparents why. They were sworn to secrecy.

Tim was waiting for his grandmother when she arrived at the front of their house to take him to the food bank. He ran outside and got into the car before she came to the front door.

He didn't want her to have another fight with his mother who was still at home talking on the telephone to a client. He buckled the car seat and said, "Good Morning. Thanks for picking me up, Grandma," as cheerily as he could fake his tone of voice to show her there was nothing wrong with him or anyone else in his household.

Shirley put the gear into drive and asked, "Are you ready for your trip?"

"Yes, I packed last night. Both Lily and I got new duffel bags for our stuff, only they aren't really duffel bags because they don't have a drawstring. They actually have wheels which makes them heavier but you can pull them instead of carrying them over your shoulder like real duffel bags."

"I'm going to miss you when you're away, Tim. You're always so full of details. You keep me well informed."

"We're only gone for two weeks."

"Still, I thought I'd have Lily staying with us to keep us company. I even got her room ready for her but I think it's nice she's getting a holiday too."

"She's saved lots of money over the years and she has a scholarship."

"I know she has. So are you going to see your Uncle Johnny?"

Tim was speechless. He'd been right. His grandmother had guessed without anyone telling her.

"You've never met my Uncle Charlie, have you?" Shirley stopped at the traffic light.

"No." Tim didn't want to say that. He felt like his grandmother had tricked him. She could do that, make him say things he didn't really mean to say. His father said she knew how to stir things up. It was a skill she had, in fact he said it was the only skill she had. It seemed a very limited skill set to Tim. He wished the light would change colour so she wouldn't have time to ask him more questions and he wouldn't have to say anything that might incriminate him. Then he remembered why he was with her and how he could quickly change the subject. "What did granddad mean by a donation in my name?"

"Just that. We're giving money to the food bank to honour your essay that made us all more aware of where our food comes from and why that matters."

"But the food bank is about giving out food, not about sourcing it."

"Yes, well, I thought maybe you would like to volunteer there with me when you get back from your family vacation? They need help and you have to earn volunteer hours."

"I was thinking I would like to volunteer at the senior's residence."

"Oh, you can do that too. Here we are." Shirley pulled into the parking lot beside the Presbyterian Church. They entered through an outside door at the back that led directly into the basement room where the food bank was housed.

When Tim was introduced to Cal Ford he thought he was looking at an older version of his Uncle Johnny only this man was thin, or more wasted looking than slim. He immediately recognized Cal as a type: wasted, migrant, reformed. Suddenly Tim felt grown-up. It was as if meeting this man in these circumstances made him fully aware of the circumstances of people's lives and what life could or could not offer. Cal asked Shirley to take a formal shot of Tim handing over the cheque.

"Tony wanted to do this quietly," she said.

"I understand, girl, but for the record, you see. I'll only show it to the members of the board. They'll want to know about this generous donation. We don't often get this amount just handed over like you folks are doing."

Tim got a close look at the cheque and the amount as they held the slip of paper between them for the photo. He wasn't shocked as he always knew his granddad had money, but still, to just be able to get your hands on five thousand spare cash was impressive.

Cal shook Tim's hand saying, "Thanks, buddy. This will come in handy to renovate the space with more refrigeration."

"Can I see the food storage area?"

"Sure, follow me."

Tim followed Cal into the adjoining kitchen that had two white refrigerators with small freezers on the top. "So I guess you need proper freezer compartments?"

"You got it. Speaking of," Cal turned to Shirley who was standing in the doorway. "You wouldn't have time to do a pick-up from Marshal's Dairy on County Road 7, would you?"

"I'd be glad to help out," Shirley said. "You can come with me, Tim."

"Sure."

"That'd be swell," Cal said. "They're short a delivery van but have some extra dairy products for us: butter, cheese, cream. You know if I can get it here before the folks come then I can distribute it today."

"You need help with that?"

"No thanks, Shirley. This is the day the good Christian men and women of St. Paul's come. They help a lot with the cleaning, too, and get set up for Sunday Service. Just tell Marshal Cal sent you."

"Will do."

Back inside the car Shirley explained to Tim that Cal was the caretaker at the church but he did a lot more than what the congregation paid him to do. "Like help out with the food bank," she said.

"That's really good of him. You seem to get along with him."

"Yes, I do," Shirley said. "He's found a home there."

"Was he homeless before?"

"He was at one time in his life. It takes having experience to really understand the situation. Except for people like you, Tim. You just know because you're so smart."

"Thanks, Grandma."

Chapter 25

The Road Trip

Once the family had the car packed Pamela got behind the wheel. Tim took the window seat behind his Mom and Lily sat across from him beside the other passenger window. Clinton turned around to look at his children. "You know in my day we didn't have seat belts. Sometimes I sat on the floor and played."

"That sounds dangerous," Lily said.

Pamela drove along the two lane paved highway that headed east out of town to the service station where they stopped to fill up with gas. Then Clinton took over driving as his wife did not like driving on the busy divided highway that went north. Lily had her driver's license but she didn't like highway driving either. Her attitude convinced Tim that when he learned to drive he would be confident enough to go anywhere in his own car.

Pamela tuned the car radio to a local station that was playing golden oldies. She smiled at Clinton who said, "A splash from the past."

Tim turned away from his parents and thought about his great grandmother who seemed to live in the past. He heard her worn-out voice. He pictured her ravaged face. He remembered her slow movements. When he'd visited her at Dellport Seniors' Residence he was somewhat shocked. He hadn't expected what he'd found, a very old lady who no longer knew who he was. He could understand why she was more attached to Uncle Johnny since he was her blood relative and she'd watched him grow up. Besides, when he'd recently come to town he'd gone to the residence to visit her. In his own way his uncle was loyal. Tim raised his voice above the road noise and radio to get his mother's attention. "What would you think if I volunteered at the senior's residence?"

Pamela turned to look at him all the while bobbing her head to the music. "That's a fine idea."

"Only Grandma has me doing volunteer work at the Food Bank."

"She does?"

"Grandpa donated money to the Food Bank in my name."

"He did?" Pamela's head stopped bobbing and she shifted her weight in her seat to turn her full body around to look at him without straining the car seat belt. "When did all this happen?"

"A couple of weeks ago."

"You didn't tell me."

"No, sorry, but Grandpa wanted to keep it quiet. He also wanted the donation to be anonymous even though he sent me with Grandma to deliver it in person. He didn't want some reporter there and have it written up in the newspaper for everyone in town to see."

Clinton chuckled. "There's been enough of that, eh?"

"Please, Clinton," Pamela said.

"Well you have to admit she's kept the local reporters busy."

"Also Grandpa didn't want people to speculate on the amount of the donation."

Clinton laughed. "That's very smart of him."

Pamela continued, "I guess his intentions are good. I mean, with everything that's happened, but you don't need to go to the food bank if you don't want to Tim."

"I just didn't know how you'd feel about me going to a place where you work."

"That's fine by me. I'm only at the seniors' residence periodically. It's not like I'm full time there. You'd do well. There are a few girls I know who go. They're older, more Lily's age. I would have suggested she get a job there but they didn't need her help. They will need help come the fall, though."

"I was thinking I could play music for them. There was an old lady playing the piano giving a recital when I went with Grandpa."

"Yes, I heard about that, but I don't think she was that old. She's the daughter of one of the residents. She's come before. I heard her play once."

"They all look old."

Clinton let out a bellow. "Ha, ha, ha."

Pamela turned away from Tim and stared at the profile of her husband. "You're not helping, Clinton." Her voice was firm, not full of understanding like she used with Tim.

"How did you find Maud?" Clinton asked ignoring his wife's reproach.

"Well she dozed off during the recital."

"That's common enough," Pamela said. "They drift in and out of awareness. Sometimes they'll doze off in the middle of a sentence. You get used to it. Don't be surprised if they die on you. More than once I've knocked on someone's door to learn they've passed away the day before or a while ago but the residence hasn't changed the name sign. I don't go to their funerals or visit their graves unless I know their families. It's too much really. I mean, how can I spend my time with them in death. I'm hired to help them in the waning years of their life. They talk about death a lot. At least, some of them do. They talk about it as if they're talking about the weather. Death is about as natural and unpredictable as the weather. One thing for sure, it happens. Every day." Pamela looked ahead. Then she turned back to Tim. "Anyway, I think you'd be great with them."

"I met Richard James. He said he used to play golf with Great-Grandma."

"Christopher's father? Yes, they did. He's good to her. He's a little sharper than most, but physically he's very feeble. You'll get used to that Tim. The ones who were strong and active in their youth aren't always like that in their old age." She turned up the volume on the car radio. "Olivia Newton-John," Pamela said. "It's 'Let's get physical'. How timely. God, I remember this pop song so well. I must have been what, sixteen, when it hit the charts."

"Good message," Clinton said tapping his hand on the steering wheel.

"You think so?" Pamela asked with a hint of irony in her voice. "Like I was saying, just because you were physical in your youth doesn't mean you'll be strong in your old age."

Clinton laughed. "So how much did he donate?"

"Clinton, Tim just said he wanted it to remain a secret. And anonymous."

"As if," Clinton said. "Everyone in Dellport knows more than they need to know about everyone and everything. They think they're entitled to know secrets. Nothing stays hidden. They especially think they should know if it involves real money like the kind your parents have."

Tim refused to say and betray his Grandpa. Turning away

from his parents Tim looked over at his sister who was oblivious to him and their parents. She was in her own world. She had on a head set that was connected to her Sony Walkman. He wondered what music she was listening to as he couldn't hear any notes escaping or wafting through the air to reach him. Lily never played music too loudly. She was way too sensible for that.

Tim looked beyond his sister at the scenery passing by her window. They were now entering the Canadian Shield, a land of great rocks, massive and striated. Other years his family had travelled here with their tents and camped on sites near pristine lakes. He liked the change of scenery and looked forward to going further north than he'd ever been.

Chapter 26

Gone Fishing

Johnny said they could find large trout in the channel in the deepest part of the lake behind a point they could see from the lodge. The surface of the water was still and so was the air. It was quiet when he'd gotten Tim and Clinton out of bed. He'd warned them the night before when they'd arrived late that he would get them up early to go fishing. Over the steady thrumming of the motor he told them he had the depths mapped which was why he could guarantee a catch. That was what brought tourists back every year. "They like it when they can take home part of the catch," he said to them while keeping his eyes ahead to where they were going.

Tim sat in the bow with his dad and looked ahead too. It was an enchanted lake surrounded by virgin land with rock cliffs and forests that went back as far as the eye could see. On the shore there were a few rocky escarpments bordered by cedar trees, but when they reached the point and turned into the channel the shoreline was sheer cliff face. Now Tim understood why it was deep here. The lodge was built on a bay that was shallow enough for the water to warm up during the day and over the summer season, shallow enough for swimming. His Uncle Johnny promised him later in the afternoon they could all go swimming.

'Fishing, boating, and swimming,' he'd said. 'What else could a man ask for in this life?'

Clinton caught the first fish, a lake trout that weighed 9 pounds. He couldn't stop laughing. Johnny made sure that his nephew caught the next one. Tim understood how his uncle made a good life as a fishing guide. "Thanks, Uncle Johnny."

"You're welcome. How be we eat this one for breakfast? Won't your mom and sister be surprised and pleased to be dished up this fresh beauty. We can smoke and can your dad's catch for you all to take home if that's okay with you, Clinton?"

"Fine by me."

"Well let's go back. No point being greedy, eh?"

With smiles on their faces Clinton and Tim once again took their seats in the bow. By now the early morning rays of sunshine dappled the surface of the lake with a silver light that bounced into the air like jewels. They soon reached the L-shaped dock where Johnny maneuvered the boat snuggly behind the front platform. As they were lifting the fish from the boat Pamela waved from the cabin and walked down the cedar chip pathway to greet them. She still hadn't gotten over how much Johnny looked like their great Uncle Charlie. They were both tall with long limbs but not too tall to be overpowering. Johnny's hair was very blonde from being so much in the sun and Charlie's was turning grey. They both had the same sparkling, small eyes.

"We're taking these beauties straight up to the lodge," Johnny said.

"Breakfast," Tim said showing his mom his catch.

Pamela walked beside her son. "Wow, that's fantastic, Tim. How'd you do that?"

"With Uncle Johnny's help."

"Naw, you didn't need my help. You're a natural."

"This one's for us to take home," Clinton said.

"Will it keep?"

Clinton laughed and stopped to let his wife and son catch up to him. "We get to smoke it; then can it."

"Really?"

"Then you'll get to taste a bit of this place after you're gone to make you want to return." Johnny took the wooden stairs two at a time. "Follow me to the kitchen, folks."

"Maybe I should go and wake up Lily," Pamela said. As she left them she passed another guest whom she greeted while singing the praises of her family's catch. She found Lily still in bed snuggled deeply under the covers in the dark of her room. Their cabin seemed like a bit of luxury in the deep woods, certainly more luxurious than anything they had experienced camping in tents. While camp grounds offered running water, shower stalls, and flush toilets to all campers in a communal building, this cabin had all these features with their own, private bathroom. It was just like their bathroom at home only here a propane tank situated outdoors heated their water and their green toilet was linked to a grey water system. "Lily," Pamela called softly.

The covers moved as Lily rolled over to her other side, turning away from her mother.

Pamela sat on the side of the bed. "Time to get up, dear."

"Can't I sleep in?" Lily mumbled. "I'm on holiday."

"Yes, but Daddy and Tim have already been out fishing with Uncle Johnny and they caught some for breakfast."

Lily rolled onto her back and pushed the blanket off her face. "Fish for breakfast?"

"Well if you want something else, just ask. You don't have to eat fish if you don't want to."

"I didn't know it would be like this."

"Like what?" Pamela slipped her thigh onto the blanket and leaned in closer to her daughter.

"It's so far away." Lily folded her forearms over the top of the blanket.

"Is that a problem?"

"It is if you want to get away."

"I think that's the point," Pamela said. "To get away. From civilization." She sat looking at her daughter wondering why Lily, who was not at all a social animal, felt this way.

"Umm," Lily said in earnest contemplation. "I guess you're right."

"Well, get up dear and come to breakfast in the lodge. Humour your father and brother."

Lily let out a long sigh. "Alright, I will."

Pamela rose and went to the window but Lily asked her not to open the blinds yet until she got dressed. As Pamela waited for her daughter, she stood on the screened front porch and stared over the lake. It was a beautiful spot. It was where she was conceived. She thought hard about that. She belonged here although her mother had never returned nor ever spoke to her about the place. Why should she feel ashamed about what happened here? Why not visit somewhere that was as innocent as a newborn baby? Why not experience nature in its element? Pamela was grateful to Johnny for having invited them and for having arranged for their special vacation. It would probably be the last one they had with Lily. The door behind her opened and Lily stepped out to join her mother. Together they walked across the rocky path to the lodge.

Once inside Lily grew animated. She hovered by her father who was preparing his catch for smoking under the guidance of

Charlie, their great uncle. They'd never met their great grandmother, Hazel. Charlie was her brother, Shirley's uncle. He was as old as the hills and looked it. His grey hair stood off his scalp like threads of wire. His tanned skin was mostly liver spots that hung off his bones like a turkey's wattle. His head nodded continuously with the shakes. She left them for the other action that was happening at the big counter in the middle of the large kitchen. Uncle Johnny had helped Tim filet the fish on the steel counter top and they were moving it to the regular counter under the cupboards where they took out a tin of flour for putting in a dish to cover the fish filets. Her uncle gave her an apron and asked her to stir the potatoes that were frying in a large, iron skillet over the burner on the large stove that had six, not four, burners. Soon she was cooking beside Tim who was frying the fish. Pamela made toast and before 8 o'clock they were all sitting down to a hardy breakfast. Everyone agreed fish tasted best when it was freshly caught.

"Can I go fishing?" Lily asked.

"Sure you can," Johnny said.

"I'll take you out later this afternoon," Charlie said. "We can go out in the canoe and catch some bass for supper in the bay."

"Cool," Tim said.

"Why, isn't that what you did?" Lily asked and stared at her brother with shameless curiosity. Why did he think she was doing something 'cool'?

"No, we went out in the down rigger and caught lake trout."

"That's what you're eating, Lily," Clinton said.

"Whatever," Lily said.

Johnny rose. "Well thanks guys for breakfast. Now I have work to do. It's going to be a brilliant day so just relax, go swimming, take a walk in the woods. But don't get lost."

"We won't," Tim called to his departing uncle.

Chapter 27

A Dark Night

"It's very dark outside." Pamela looked directly ahead. "I can sort of see the outline of the trees. They're so tall. Taller than any trees I've ever seen. Majestic."

"Yes," Charlie said. "They are and then, when you go further north, they get smaller until there are no trees left."

"Have you been that far north?"

"Once about a decade ago. Maybe now that you've come this far you'll want to go there sometime?"

"Maybe," Pamela said softly.

"By next weekend the nights will be pitch black. Last weekend we had a full moon. Some of the guests went canoing right around this time."

"That would be something to experience." Pamela turned her head to look at her old uncle curious about his life, about all she didn't know, about the things he knew that she didn't. "Actually I'm happy to have finally come this far."

Charlie nodded his head at her. "Darlin', I am too. Last time I saw you, you was only two years old. That was a long time ago."

"Over forty years." They were sitting together in the screened in porch separated from the others by a log wall.

Pamela felt now was her opportunity. "So you knew my real father?"

"I certainly did."

"Can you tell me about him?"

"Sure. What do you want to know?"

"Everything. What he did. What he looked like."

"Monty was a guy with big hands, large knuckles, and strong muscles. He was a good worker. We didn't have all these modern conveniences back then. He could swing an axe, that one. Your mother fell for him right away."

"Did she? She doesn't even talk about him now. Refuses to let me find him." Pamela placed her forearms on the wooden chair rest and drummed her fingers.

"Johnny says you're trying."

"Yes."

"You'll find him. Do you want some help?"

Pamela looked at him. "Can you help?"

"I can ask around. There's a pair live hardscrabble in the bush who were here the same time as him. There's another guy's got his own fishing place on a remote lake who knew him back then. Can't hurt to ask."

"Maybe there's hope."

"There's always hope, Pammy." He laughed. "That's what your dad called you. Pammy. He sure was broke up when your mom took you away. Your mom was right confused back then. She didn't know what she wanted. Caused a great rift in the family I guess. I never saw my sister again, you know? Hazel blamed me. Well, she had to blame someone. She'd had a hard time raising Shirley after Robert and Ian were killed in that boating accident. Wasn't like there was insurance back then. I helped her. At least I sent money. That's why Shirley thought she could come to me. She thought I was the one with the bucks. Didn't have much back then but don't need much to live here. I don't think she was disappointed in me. At her age a teenager likes to find freedom. She was just after some freedom from the constraints of her mother. Then she had you. I was a witness at their wedding, you know. It was what was called back then a shot gun wedding. Oh, we had a blast. There was a lot of partying went on in them days. People drank a lot more then. Hard stuff. Not like now. Most of the guests drink beer but some prefer wine. It's changed. Yep."

Pamela watched Charlie's head move up and down in agreement with all that he'd said. She was amazed. She'd heard more from him in one sitting than she'd heard in a lifetime from her mother. "So you knew me as a baby?"

"I sure did. You were a beautiful baby. Then Hazel came and took you both away. Set the divorce in motion. Didn't take much. Monty never contested it. He had a temper. He knew it. Still, made him sad, though. I hope you's find him."

"I wonder if Mom went out in the boat when she came here? It's only that she wouldn't ride in a boat and was so adamant about none of us going out in boats."

"Because of Ian and your granddad?"

"Yes, that must have been a terrible tragedy?"

"I guess you never knew your granddad? But do you remember your grandma?"

"Yes, I do, a little."

"Johnny didn't know her. I didn't hear about her passing on until after her funeral."

"That's very sad," Pamela said. "She didn't tell you?"

"No, it was one of the Montgomery's who sent me a notice."

"Really? We don't have much to do with them."

"They're your cousins. Johnny knows them."

"Yes, he liked hanging out at their marina. I thought it was just because Mom said not to go there. Johnny always liked to defy authority."

Charlie laughed. "Ain't that the way? Are they still on Lake Street?"

"Yes, Montgomery's Marina. Just down from the pier. It took a lot for Dad to convince Mom to even go on a cruise."

Charlie nodded. "So they've travelled, have they?"

"Yes, everywhere. They cruised the world with two other couples, Mom's friend, Linda Leach and her husband who's now dead, and Dad's good friend, Ramsey Reisch and his wife, Rose."

"She's been right spoiled, your mother."

"Yes, in later life, but not when she was young, right?"

"No, not then. Our family never had much. After the depression then there was the war."

"Do you remember that time?"

Charlie nodded some more. "Yep, sure I do. I was a kid watchin' 'em all head overseas. Including your grandaddy, Robert. I guess you'd say he came back shell shocked."

"P.T.S.D.," Pamela said.

"That's what they's call it now." Charlie turned to Pamela. "I guess you's know all about that in your line of work?"

"Post Traumatic Stress Disorder? Yes, that and a lot of other stresses."

"You see, Monty was a draft dodger."

"He was?"

"Yep. He didn't want to go to that Vietnam war. Same with the pair of them I was telling you about who live in the woods but they didn't return to the States."

"So do you think Monty did?" Pamela blinked the tears from

her eyes. Not a bad man then. A draft dodger. Did this partly explain why her grandmother hated him? How could she like a draft dodger when her own husband had suffered as a vet from the Second World War?

Charlie pursed his lips. "I reckon that may be the case. When President Ford granted clemency in 1974, Monty started thinking about returning and then Carter granted a full pardon at the beginning of his term in 1977. I think by then Monty was ready to return to his own family in the States."

A loud laugh from the interior of the cabin reached them. They stood and went inside together. "What's all this then?" Charlie asked.

Lily piped up. "Uncle Johnny beat Tim at cribbage."

"What's so funny?" Pamela asked.

"Tim's so tired he nodded off in the middle of playing. It was easy beating him."

"Maybe you should go to bed, Tim," Pamela said. "You've been up since dawn."

Clinton laughed. "All this fresh air. Fishing. Swimming."

"That's not it," Tim said in his own defense.

"It's getting late," Pamela said. "Time to turn in."

Johnny rose. "Well, we should all go back to our own cabins. It's been a great day having you here with us enjoying the place."

"It sure has," Clinton said.

"I'm so glad we came," Pamela said as she rose on her tip toes to kiss her brother goodnight. She walked him and her uncle out and stood inside the screened-in porch watching them depart. Her eyes followed the beams of light from their flashlights that zigzagged over the ground. Pamela inhaled deeply. She felt content. Charlie had given her what she wanted: a story about her beginnings, hope that she would find her father, and a place to call home. She belonged here. Not as Pamela Croft. Not even as Pamela Palmer, but as Pamela Caragiale. When the children were in bed she confided in Clinton. "Monty was a draft dodger."

"He was? An American then?"

"Yes, and that's not all. There are still draft dodgers living up here and Charlie thinks they can help us find him."

"So maybe not a bad man?"

"Maybe not. Johnny's not so bad, either, is he?"

"As long as he's up here," Clinton said.

Chapter 28

A Summer Cold

"Feed a cold. Starve a fever."

Shirley opened her groggy eyes. Above her bed Tony stood with a tray in his hands. "Achoo," she sneezed leaning over the side of the bed where the spray of germs fell through the air.

"Sorry, dear, I can't reach the Kleenex box while holding this."

Shirley fell against her pillow that was propped against the headboard. She had spent the night with her head slightly raised to help her passages drain. Last night she'd started shivering before going to bed early in the evening. She'd had a miserable night. Now she reached for a tissue and blew her nose. Then she propped herself up taller so Tony could place the tray over her lap. Then he lifted the garbage basket so she could throw the used tissue away. "Thanks." Shirley heard the word echo in her ear. It sounded like 'dansh'. She looked down at the tray which held a tall glass of orange juice, a smaller glass of water, a boiled egg in an egg cup and a small plate with buttered toast.

"See. I can boil an egg."

Shirley smiled. "This is very sweet. Just what the doctor ordered."

"I'll have my shower now."

Shirley watched Tony retreat into the en suite bathroom and close the door. He had spent the night in the room across the hall, the one she'd prepared for Lily thinking she would have her granddaughter stay while the rest of her family went on holiday. Shirley picked up the knife and cracked the top off the egg. A bit of dark yellow yolk oozed over the sides of the brown shell. Since shopping at the Farmers' Market she'd been purchasing local organic eggs that had colour and taste. Only this morning the egg could have been made out of cardboard. Her taste buds were gone, yet she was hungry so she dutifully ate everything Tony had prepared while listening to the shower running. How had she gotten a cold, she wondered. It wasn't from her husband. He was still cheery and healthy. She hoped no one else in the family had her cold that could be spoiling their holiday. When Tony came out of the shower and dressed for his golf game she asked him to inquire if anyone else had a cold.

Tony placed the glass of water on her night stand then lifted the tray. "Maybe you got it from working at the food bank."

"You think so?"

"Seems most likely. The people who use that place probably aren't as healthy as the people at the golf course. Maybe you should start washing your hands when you come home from there."

"You sound like my late mother."

"Mother always knows best. Just to remind you the guy who's going to clean the floors comes today. Shall I leave the door open or will you get up to let him in? He should be here shortly. I could wait but he could be late and then we'd miss our tee-off time. I don't want to hold up our game."

Shirley remembered that Tony had arranged for one of the window washers to come to scrub floors downstairs. "Leave the door open for him." She couldn't picture herself getting out of bed to answer the door. As Tony left she drifted off. Later she heard a commotion downstairs which gave her a fright but then she remembered about the cleaner coming. Propping herself up in bed she reached for the glass of water. She was thirsty and downed the contents. Then she got out of bed and went into the bathroom. It still smelled of the soap Tony used. The room was gleaming clean. She had cleaned it when she'd prepared the room and main bathroom for Lily. What she did for her grandchildren. A lot more housework than she'd done in years. The tinkle of pee echoed in the small room which for some reason left her embarrassed. She decided not to flush the toilet. Besides, she reasoned, the water pressure was low and she didn't want to interfere with the cleaner and his work. It had been a dry summer and there had been a water advisory warning to limit usage. Before getting back into bed she retrieved her glass and filled it. She must have drifted off again in bed because the next thing she was aware of was Tony coming quietly into the room to ask if she needed anything. He said he'd bring her some lunch. Before leaving he handed her the local paper that was wrapped in an orange tinted plastic bag that was tied closed. "Since when did they deliver the paper like this?" she asked.

"Since the newspaper decided to protect the paper from getting wet when they deliver it to the sidewalk."

"The sidewalk?"

"Yes. It speeds up delivery to throw it on the sidewalk rather than walk up the sidewalk and deliver it to our doorstep."

"Really?"

"I know it sounds a waste but there you have it. Apparently they're having trouble finding delivery boys to do the job."

"I remember when Johnny had a route."

"He did." Tony didn't remind her that he had had to go out with Johnny to do the delivery because Johnny would get sidetracked and end up at the marina where there was far more fun to be had than on the paper route.

"So do the people at the newspaper office think it's going to rain?"

"They don't think, Shirley. They're no longer paid to think. They've been bought out by a large conglomerate. Back shortly."

After untying the orange plastic bag, Shirley pulled out the paper. She stuffed the flyers back into the narrow bag. The front page pictured a sprinkler with a caption saying that this practice was contrary to municipal regulations. Without bothering to read the article she opened the newspaper to the middle where what was happening around town and throughout the county were listed. An ad caught her attention. There was the movie she wanted to see. 'Rocky Horror Picture Show' was the movie she'd heard about from way back that had been a hit cult film. It was coming to the revue cinema in a neighbouring town that attracted tourists in the summer to its beach. Shirley thought she would take Lily to that cinema as a treat but hadn't mentioned it after learning that her granddaughter wasn't coming to stay. How could she go by herself? Who else would go with her? How could she go with a cold?

Then she remembered Linda. Why hadn't she heard from Linda lately? It had been ages since they talked. Picking up the phone from the bedside table she put it to her ear but there was no dial tone. Then she remembered that Tony had pulled the cord so the ringing would not disturb her sleep. Carefully she eased herself out of bed and reaching for the transparent cord reconnected it. Then she speed dialed the number. "'ello Linda."

"Who's this?"

"It's Sirley."

"You don't sound like Shirley."

"I have a cold."

"Ah, poor you. That's too bad catching a cold in summer."

"Tony said it's because I volunteer at the food bank."

"Yes, I heard you were doing that."

"Listen Linda, do you want to go to a movie at the revue cinema?"

"Shirley, you have a cold. You're not going anywhere."

"I might be over it in time. There's a movie I want to see. It's listed in the paper."

"I don't think I got my paper."

"Linda, check your sidewalk. Tony says they no longer deliver the paper to your front door."

"You mean I have to go outside to the sidewalk to pick up the paper?"

"That's right, Linda."

"But how will I manage in the winter?"

"Linda, don't worry about that now. Do you want to come with me?"

"I don't know, Shirley. Maybe this isn't a good idea driving out of town."

"What do you mean?" Shirley had never heard Linda express doubt about her proposed outings. Had something happened? "Are you all right, Linda?"

"Yes, Shirley. I am. You're the one with the cold. People with colds shouldn't go out in public. Besides, I don't want to get into any more trouble."

"What do you mean? Trouble?"

"I always seem to get into trouble with you."

"Linda, what happened to just having fun?"

"Maybe we're getting too old for that."

"Nonsense."

"You take care of that cold, Shirley. Can I bring you anything?"

"No, thanks. Tony's preparing my lunch as we speak."

She hung up the phone disappointed that Linda had not been more congenial. Why was Linda suddenly feeling old? Who else would be game to go to that movie? She knew she couldn't ask Tony. Firstly, he'd say what Linda had. Secondly, he'd never agree to see something so off-the-wall. More to the point, she wanted to go with a female.

While scheming, Shirley scanned the other listings. Soon Tony returned with the tray. "You're spoiling me," she said. She shoved the paper aside. "I'm feeling so much better."

"You sound better," he said.

"I was just reading about what's happening in the paper. There's no need to miss anything."

"Well I'm going."

"You are?"

"Yes," Tony said. "I want to hear what the professor has to say."

"The professor?" Shirley asked.

"Yes, Robert McGhee." Tony picked up the paper. "Tonight. At 7:30. Sponsored by Rotary."

"Yes, tonight," Shirley said feeling her plan slip away.

Tony read, "Ice was crucial to the peopling of North America. The last Ice Age lowered sea levels so that Asia and Alaska were joined."

Shirley stopped listening. The Ice Age? Was Tony serious? This professor was coming in the middle of the summer to talk about ice? Would this make everyone feel cooler? All of a sudden she felt cooler. Shirley started to shiver.

Tony looked over at her. "Are you cold?"

"No, I just need something to eat," she said. Shirley picked up the spoon and stirred the chicken noodle soup. She put the warm liquid to her lips. Despite her best efforts a little spilled. She picked up the paper napkin and wiped her lips.

"I don't think you're ready to go anywhere," Tony said.

"You're probably right," Shirley said. She hated to admit that she should remain in bed, not because she would miss the talk by Professor Robert McGhee, but because she wouldn't get to see 'The Rocky Horror Picture Show'. It was the movie that was on her bucket list. It was a movie with a reputation. It was a movie like no other movie in cinema history. Tonight would have been her one chance to see it while she was still sixty. Soon she would turn sixty-one and it would be too late. She'd had six things on her bucket list and so far she'd only done a few. Now she would have to add the movie 'The Rocky Horror Picture Show' to her list of failed attempts. Growing old really was the pits.

Chapter 29

Family First

It so happened that Pamela's first client after her holidays lived at Dellport Retirement Residence. However, the appointment wasn't until 11 am and, instead of using her time for paper work, she decided to go see her mother. Tony answered the door.

"Your mother's still sleeping," he said quietly and ushered her into the kitchen.

"My," Pamela said, "your house is so clean."

Tony explained who had helped them with the grunt housework like cleaning floors. Then he explained, "Your mother has been sick."

"She has?"

"Nothing serious. Just a cold."

"A cold in the summer? That's unusual."

"She got quite run down which is also unusual. Can you wait or come back later?"

Pamela sat down. "I want to share with her what I discovered when we were away."

Tony sat kitty corner to her at the kitchen table. "Is it anything you can share with me?"

"It's just," Pamela began. "I don't know where to start. She's always been so critical of me. Does she hate me like she hates my birth father?"

"Why no, Pamela. She thinks the world of you. Your mother admires you."

"Are you sure?"

"Yes," Tony said gently. He reached over and pulled her head closer giving her a peck on the top of her head. "She loves you." Tony felt flustered. He was unused to such intimacy with Pamela as a grown woman. "I can't speak for your mother but I know she loves your entire family, Lily and Tim. Even Clinton."

Pamela laughed. "That I find hard to believe."

Tony pulled himself away from Pamela. "You're family. Family comes first."

"Yes, I know, but," Pamela looked directly into Tony's eyes, "do you know I'm trying to find Monty."

"Really? Now why would you want to do that?"

"You just said 'family comes first'."

"I meant to us, to me and your mother. You're our family and you come first."

"Uncle Charlie thinks he can help me."

Tony stared at her in silence.

"I just want to know who he is."

"Of course you do, dear. It's only natural." Tony smiled with closed lips. "That's a good plan, Pamela. Asking him. It's just something of a surprise."

"You don't mind?" Pamela asked.

"No, I guess not. Sometimes it helps to know the truth. It never helps to believe lies."

"Did you know he was a draft dodger from the Vietnam War?"

"I did," Tony said firmly. "That was something that rankled Hazel and not something she wanted the town to know. She only told me after I married Shirley. Hazel conspired to paint Monty in the worst light so that people would make their own assumptions and judge him badly. She knew how to manipulate popular opinion."

"Hazel did? My Grandmother?"

"Yes," Tony said.

"The gossip mill. But I believed the gossip. Why was I made to feel so ashamed of my roots? Why didn't she know how it would hurt me?"

"What Shirley knows is how it hurt her. Hazel had ambitions for her. Especially after losing her son. She tried hard with her daughter but, let's face it, Shirley is no academic. She remembers what people say in conversation, but only if they're talking about other people, not ideas."

"That's a curious way of putting it," Pamela said. She reflected on this for a moment. "I guess she's not going to change?"

"Probably not."

"I came here to confide in her about what I am doing."

"I think," Tony began cautiously, "you must know that she knows where you went and it is as much as she can stand that you were with Johnny on a family holiday. That he even invited you and not her. And that you got to be there, at the place where she'd escaped to when she couldn't bear things. She found love there. She had you."

Pamela knew Tony had an unwavering Christian faith, only now she understood that, unlike her mother, he was not a fundamentalist. He suffered and in his suffering offered true charity. "Thank you."

"No, thank you for trusting in me to share your problems. It helps to hand your problems over sometimes."

"Should I not say anything to her then?"

"No, don't. This is your problem for now and your journey. When you find him that will be soon enough to let her know what you've discovered."

Chapter 30

Death

In August the weather changed. A record was set on June 6 as the hottest day. That was followed by a very hot month of July, but by the second week of August a cold spell settled in which some welcomed as a relief from the brutally warm summer weather but which others saw as a cheat by making the summer season too short. When the cold continued into a second week everyone started complaining. Tony said that was typical behaviour. People forgot how they'd suffered in July, but no one ever forgot how to complain about the weather.

The month of February is typically a cold month and the coldest day so far that year had been February 11. Also, typically, more people died in the coldest month, and as if the cold reminded people of the inevitable, old people started dying. The latest to pass away was Dorothy Baxter. She was in her ninetieth year.

On Saturday morning, August 15, Shirley and Tony got ready to attend the funeral. They raided their fall wardrobe. Shirley said Dorothy was being most accommodating picking such cool temperatures because no one would have any problems finding dark clothes to wear. They had met the new reverend who was named Brathwaite last month. At the time they were surprised by his boyish looks. He was more than simply young. Shirley and Tony had agreed that youthful professionals were getting younger by the day which clearly made them feel older by the day. Tony had also introduced Shirley to the reverend's wife, Nia, who was the new bank manager.

Tony parked the car in the lot attached to St. Anthony United Church. There were plenty of spots. "This will be a small affair," Tony said. They could see the Catholic church from the parking lot where a very large funeral was being held. They'd read Hank Nicholl's obituary in the local paper alongside Dorothy's. He was their age which made them take pause.

Inside the church they took a program from the usher who led them to the second pew from the front. "Thank you," Tony said in hushed tones to Matthew, the reverend's son.

Sitting beside her husband Shirley silently read the program. On the front was a picture of Dorothy when she was a young woman, mature, adult, but not a likeness to the person they recently remembered. Shirley thought why not. Best to be remembered in one's prime. She opened the program to the order of service and followed along with the prayers and hymns. Dorothy was a very private person and no one in the family spoke. It was all very formal and short. Shirley thought why not. She'd had a long life so why have a long funeral? Before long they were back outside in the cold August day. Shirley and Tony followed the few cars to the cemetery where Dorothy's only daughter, Julie, did speak about her mother. She ended with, "She will forever be with us in our loving hearts."

As the casket was lowered Julie threw a bouquet of flowers into the grave. Her brother did the same. They had postponed the funeral service until he could arrive from Hong Kong. Then Julie invited everyone to the house.

Before heading to the car Tony and Shirley took a detour to visit her parents' grave. There were three names on the tall granite headstone: Robert Montgomery, Ian Montgomery, and Hazel (Long) Montgomery. Shirley looked at the dates and thought how short lived her brother's life was. He was just a boy when he died. Her mother was born in 1928 and also died way too young. "She never reached old age," Shirley said.

"No, she missed out on that," Tony said knowing he was stating the obvious but feeling how unfair it was.

They passed the war vets cemetery on their way back to the car. "I'm glad my Dad's not buried here," Shirley said. "It's better to be in a family plot."

"I think the vet plot is for those who died serving," Tony said.

Shirley stopped walking and stared at him. "Of course. What was I thinking?"

"You were thinking of your parents."

"I was but sometimes I seem to get confused. It worries me."

"Don't be worried, Shirley. You just get overwhelmed. That's natural." He put his hand on her elbow and directed her to the parked car.

In the car Shirley said, "That was the kind of funeral I want to have. Simple. Short."

"Yes, I agree," Tony said while looking in the rear view mirror before backing up and then driving out of the parking lot. "We should plan our funerals, Shirley. It's something I've been meaning to do."

"What? Now? You think so?"

"Yes, we should talk about the service. Set out what prayers and music and hymns we want. You never know. Look at Hank Nicholl. Here today. Gone tomorrow."

"Well I guess that's what people do though it seems too soon to me."

"Yes and no. Nothing like being prepared. We're not all going to live to be ninety like Dorothy Baxter."

"What about Maud? Does she have a service ready."

"Well, she has spoken to me about her wishes, but you're right. I should begin with her and formally record how she wants things done."

Once again Shirley looked at the black and white formal photograph of young Dorothy Baxter on the front of the obituary program. You couldn't say she was a pretty woman, more handsome. Her hair was swept off her face in a broad wave, the fashion from the forties. Her forehead was very high, like Julie's. They had brains, those women. The younger Dorothy didn't have much of a neck and yet Shirley distinctly remembered seeing her neck when they met at the Farmers' Market. It was thin and wrinkled. In the picture she wore a dress with a scoop neck that showed her smooth skin. Reviewing the order of service she noted some passages that the young Reverend Brathwaite had read. "He has a deep voice."

"You mean Brathwaite?"

Shirley nodded.

"Yes," Tony said confirming aloud Shirley's answer. "He seems very suited to his position. Enough gravitas to overcome his youthful looks."

Shirley raised her eyebrows. Trust Tony to use big words when the topic turned serious. "I wonder if Dorothy ever went to visit Maud?"

"She did. Christopher took her. Not that Maud remembers the visit."

"No? Too bad." Shirley thought about Maud who would

probably be the next in line to go. Her own mother had died too young, and yet, here was Maud still alive but unable to remember much except the past. She was no longer at home but living in a residence. Where was the quality of life in living like that? A hard call, but Shirley guessed her own mother wouldn't have wanted to live to such a ripe old age if it meant being dependent. She'd spent too many years in her adult life dependent on others. Like Hank Nicholls her mother died before reaching seventy. Hers was a stressful life, too. In a different way from Hank's, but nonetheless, full of stress. She'd always worried. Maybe that was the key, to not worry. Why worry? Be happy. What was it Bob Marley sang? 'In every life we have a little trouble but when you worry you make it double.' The tune ran around her head. Shirley felt like singing it aloud but thought better of it. Now was not the time.

Chapter 31

Goodbye and Good Luck

A week later Shirley and Tony hosted a family dinner at the golf club in honour of their granddaughter. The club was quiet that evening: no tournaments, no wedding receptions, no conventions; in other words, no public, just a few members sitting around tables. Tony had reserved the large round table in the middle of the room for six. Lily wore her prom dress which her grandfather admired saying he'd seen the photographs of her wearing it and was glad she'd honoured the occasion by once again putting it on. "Thanks," she said blushing.

"Shall I order some champagne?" Tony asked when they were all seated.

Lily giggled. Pamela turned to her daughter saying that would be nice for everyone.

"Me, too?" Tim asked.

"Why not?" Shirley said. "It's only a little bit for a toast."

As the waiter came around the table handing out menus Tony ordered a bottle of Laurent-Perrier Champagne. When Clinton opened his menu he whistled, then said that Shirley and Tony must be expecting to spend the balance of their chit in one sitting.

"Chit?" Tim looked at his dad. "What's that?"

"Please," Pamela said lowering her menu and looking directly over at her husband.

"What?" Clinton asked his wife.

"Tell me," Tim said.

"What's the fuss?" Shirley asked. "Your grandfather and I have a chit with the golf club because we're members."

"It's part of the annual dues or fees," Tony said needing to clarify for Tim as he still had an inquisitive look on his face. "Like a promissory note for a sum owed for food and drink, and, no, we are not spending the balance of our chit because it was spent ages ago. We've been eating here more often than usual this summer."

Without taking her eyes off the menu Pamela asked if that was because Felicia was gone.

"Now who's being impolite?" Clinton asked.

Pamela made a face at her husband by lowering her chin and staring at him from the top of her eyeballs.

"Children," Shirley said. "We're here for Lily, remember?"

"Sorry, mother," Pamela said.

"I heard they're moving," Clinton said.

"Who's moving?" Shirley asked.

"Felicia and Paolo."

"Max said something about that," Tony said.

"He did?" Shirley asked. "When did this happen?"

"Last week."

"He didn't say anything to me when he made his delivery to the food bank."

"Well, he wouldn't."

"How's it going at the food bank, Grandma?" Tim asked.

"Sorry to say I missed some hours when I had a cold last month so I have to make up some time but I think I might keep at it even after I've completed my community service. I get along well with Cal and I can see we're making a difference. What about you, Tim? How do you like volunteering at the retirement residence?"

"It's great," Tim said. "Though Great-Grandma still thinks I'm Uncle Johnny. Her friends have stopped trying to correct her. I don't mind because Uncle Johnny went to visit her when he was here so that must have sparked her memory of him."

"Mmm," Shirley said returning her eyes to scan the menu which she knew by heart.

Clinton looked over at Tim and put his finger over his lips to stay quiet about Johnny.

The waiter returned with the bottle of champagne which he showed to Tony. A young waitress set six flutes on the table and smiled at Lily who quietly said 'Hi'. After the waiter popped the cork he filled the glasses which the waitress delivered to each family member before departing. Tony raised his glass and waited for everyone to follow suit. "To Lily," he said.

"To Lily," the others echoed.

"Goodbye and good luck," Clinton said before taking a sip.

Lily shrugged her shoulders.

"Drink up," Shirley said to her granddaughter.

"Thanks everyone."

"We wish you every success in getting a degree," Pamela said.

"That's right," Clinton said. "Study hard and get good grades."

"Yes," Pamela said. "We expect you to continue, Lily."

Tony said, "After your undergraduate studies you can think about what you want to do in post graduate studies."

"You'll be a professional student," Tim said.

"No, we just want you to go further than me and your Mom did."

"Why?" Shirley asked. "You both have good jobs."

"Yes, but we only have college diplomas. Lily's bright enough to get a degree and we want to support her all the way."

"Pamela, we supported you."

"I know you did, Mom, but only for a couple of years at

college. You made it very clear I didn't have to bust a gut or break the bank."

"I did? I thought you were happy not to have to leave town once they opened the satellite campus right here."

"Yes, it was convenient, but we have different ambitions for Lily."

"I'll drink to that," Tony said raising his glass. He took a swallow. "You, too, Tim," he said tipping his glass at his grandson. "You know you have our support. Financial as well. What else are we going to do with our money?"

Tim nearly blurted out that he could give donations to other places than the food bank but he managed to censor himself and vocalized a long 'Ohhh' before closing his mouth.

"Of course we have ambitions for our grandchildren, too," Shirley said. She finished the bubbly in her flute.

Tim started to hiccup.

The adults chuckled.

The waiter returned and asked them if they were ready to order. Clinton asked if there were any specials but there weren't. "Only what's listed on the menu, sir."

"This isn't The Bletch," Pamela said, "where they write the daily specials on a blackboard that changes every day."

"Actually it's pretty much the same menu every day here," Tony said.

Asking the waiter to bring some water Tony said they would be ready to order when he returned.

After the waiter departed Clinton said he was going to have the prime rib roast with all the fixings. "I bet it's so tender it'll melt in my mouth like butter. Heh, did you hear Hank Nicholls died?" he asked

"Yes," Shirley said. "His funeral was the same day as Dorothy Baxter's."

"Which we attended," Tony said.

"So did Richard James. I saw him last weekend when he

came back to the seniors' residence. He told Great-Grandma and she wanted to know why she hadn't gone."

Shirley and Tony looked at one another. "Maybe we shouldn't have assumed she wouldn't have known what was going on," Shirley said.

"No, you shouldn't have," Pamela said. "It's the past they remember best."

"Bad call," Tony said. "We won't make that mistake again."

"So you know Paolo is back?" Clinton asked.

"Yes, he's put the house up for sale." Tony studied the menu.

"I think I'll have the pickerel. Can I have fries with that instead of mashed potatoes?" Tim asked.

"Sure you can," Shirley said. "I order that all the time but today I'm going to have the roast chicken with the local yellow and green beans."

"Me, too," Lily said.

"I'll have the pickerel but with the mash," Pamela said.

Remembering what everyone wanted Tony ordered for them saying at the end that he and Clinton were both having the beef. The young waitress poured water while the waiter wrote out the food orders. Then he went around the table picking up the large menus while asking everyone if they wanted soup or salad to start.

"Have you all had a nice day?" Shirley asked.

"Since the weather has finally returned to seasonably warm temperatures," Clinton said, "I cut the grass which is not something I usually had to do at the end of August but the grass is still growing."

Pamela said, "I went for a walk with a friend and we had a cold drink at the beach."

"I played games on my computer after visiting the seniors' home. I rode my bike in case anyone thinks I've been sedentary all day," Tim said.

"As usual I walked the therapy dogs," Lily said.

"That's been a great experience for you," Tony said.

"I guess."

"You don't sound too enthusiastic," Shirley said.

"It was good experience because I learned that I don't want to work with animals. Since we've never had a dog I thought I might see if I liked animals and I do but not enough to be a vet or anything."

"You liked visiting patients, though," Pamela said, "with the dogs."

"Yes, but I don't want to be a nurse. Maybe a social worker. I can switch to a masters program after three years so now that's my goal. The counselor said I might consider speech therapy since I like languages as well as maths and sciences. I'll just have to see how it goes."

"You still have to be good at computers," Tim said.

"For sure," Pamela said. "Everyone has to become computer literate now."

"That's true. Same for me at work. In any government position. Even the cops," Clinton said.

"And you'd know, eh, Dad?"

"Tim, remember you're on your own with us in a week's time."

"So you keep threatening."

"It's going to be different," Shirley said.

Pamela angled her head in the direction of her daughter. "I'm going to miss you."

"We all will," Tony said. "Never mind, you'll be back to visit before you know it."

The waiter served Clinton and Tim a bowl of soup and the waitress put salads in front of the three females. She smiled again at Lily.

"Do you know that girl?" Shirley asked.

"Yes, she was in my class. Do you remember her from the prom?"

"Oh, right, I recognize her now. She knew the names of all the songs. So what is she doing next year?"

"She has to save up for a year before enrolling in school."

Tony looked up at the waiter who brought him a salad. "Thanks for remembering not to put the dressing on."

"Why don't you like the salad dressing, Grandpa?" Lily asked.

"They put way too much on for my taste."

"I like this dressing," Pamela said. "It has balsamic vinegar in it."

"Definitely don't like that kind," Tony said.

"And raspberries," Tim said. "Why do they put raspberries on salad? I'm going to have them for dessert."

"Oh you saw the dessert menu already, did you?" Pamela asked.

"Yes, they have chocolate cake with raspberries and ice cream."

After the main course everyone but Clinton ordered what Tim wanted. "I'm not a chocolate eater," he said. "Never was. I know everyone claims it's healthy though it sounds suspicious to me. Just another food fad."

"They make a nice rice pudding," Tony said clamping his forearms over his belly.

"Crazy," Tim said. "Rice for dessert and raspberries on salads."

"Grains and fruit. Is rice a grain?" Clinton asked looking perplexed. He scanned around the table seeking an answer.

"Yes, it's the grain of the grass," Tony said confirming his confusion.

"Aren't we lucky we have such exotic choices?"

Tim shook his head hard in agreement. "We are, Grandma."

"Well it was that or the apple pie."

"I was thinking of ordering that," Tony said, "but I'm too full. The cake's a lot lighter than the pastry. They serve generous portions here."

"We certainly don't go hungry," Shirley said.

"Even if you can't cook," Lily said.

"Lily," Pamela admonished.

"Sorry, Grandma, I didn't mean to insult you, but I don't like to cook either and I hope I find a boy who likes to cook so he can take on that role then I can do other things."

"Like study," Tim said. "No guy's going to cook for you so you can study."

"I wouldn't be too sure, buddy," Clinton said.

"Tim, your father used to cook for me when I was studying to upgrade my qualifications."

"He did?"

"Yeah, you just don't remember because you weren't born then."

The waitress arrived with the rice pudding followed by the waiter with a tray full of cake. "Let them eat cake," Lily said when served.

"Who said that?"

"Marie Antoinette, Grandma."

"Before they cut off her head," Clinton said.

"She married Louis XVI when he was dauphin."

"Dauphin?"

"The eldest son of the King of France, Shirley," Tony said. "But it may not have been her who said 'Let them eat cake'. What she actually said during the famine when there were wide food shortages in France was 'Let them eat brioche'. Either way she was insensitive to the hungry masses. But I'm glad they're still teaching you history, Lily."

"Actually, I learned that in an essay I did for French class so

I knew it was 'Qu'ils mangent de la brioche' but it's traditionally translated as 'Let them eat cake'."

Shirley sighed. "I can see you're ready for further education. You'll be able to have conversations with your Grandpa, especially if you're interested in the ice age."

The waiter brought around a carafe of coffee. The waitress followed him and poured tea for those who didn't want coffee. At the end of the meal the waiter came over to Tony to have him sign the bill. By then everyone seemed mellow and they got up quietly to leave thanking the waiter and waitress on their way outside. It was a warm August night. They walked in pairs to their cars: Tony with Tim, Shirley with Lily, Clinton with Pamela. Above them the stars twinkled brightly. "There's the Big Dipper," Clinton said stopping and pointing.

The others stopped on the gravel parking lot and looked up. "The Milky Way," Tim said.

"A meteor," Lily said excitedly. "Did you see the meteor streak across the sky?"

"Yes," Tony said.

"Oh, I missed it," Shirley said.

Together they stood in reverential awe under the night sky lit up by half a moon. Above them the enormity of the galaxy impressed them with its lights in the near and far distance, with its expanse of unknowns, with its silence. Shirley broke the silence by giving her granddaughter a hug who in turn thanked her and her grandpa for dinner. Clinton shook Tony's hand and thanked Shirley. Tim followed his father's example. Pamela gave her father then her mother a hug in thanks. The two women held onto each other a moment longer, both struck by the otherness of their blood relative. Under the vastness of what they could see overhead was the minutiae of their separate beings. The last thing Shirley said before closing the car door was, "Have a safe journey."

Chapter 32

Crash

On the Monday morning of September 15 Shirley thought she should do laundry. She thought she should make it a habit to do laundry on Mondays just like her mother who had always done laundry on Mondays. Hazel said it was a habit left over from days living on the family farm when they would have a Sunday roast and not have to cook on Mondays because they would eat leftovers which freed them to do laundry all day because that was what it took back then. It took all day to do the laundry. Shirley figured it will take her less than half a day because she had an automatic washer and dryer. Felicia used to dry her own laundry at her house on a line but Shirley said she didn't want laundry hanging out for the neighbourhood to see so she never followed Felicia's example. Shirley thought since Felicia wasn't coming back east she should get into some routine to look after her own household. She needed some order so she stripped the bed and took the sheets downstairs but as she was carrying them the phone rang. Feeling the urgency of the ring she dropped the sheets onto the floor and picked up the land line. It was Pamela asking her to come over. "I'm just starting the laundry."

"Oh, well, come over as soon as you've started it."

"Tony doesn't like me to leave machines running when no one is at home. He thinks the dishwasher and washing machine will flood or the dryer or oven will catch fire and there will be no one to save the house from disaster and then we could have a fight on our hands with the insurance people."

"Then come over before you start the laundry."

Shirley sighed and put her hand over her eyes to better pay attention to her daughter. She tried to picture Pamela on the other end of the line alone in her house without children to occupy her time. "What's the hurry?"

"Just something I have to show you."

"Can it wait?"

"No, not really."

Shirley looked down at the floor where the sheets were lumped into a pile. Really, what was so important about doing laundry? If her daughter needed her she should go to her so she agreed to come. On the drive over Shirley thought about all that hadn't been said between them. Since returning from the lodge where Shirley knew the family had gone she had been uncharacteristically quiet: no questions, no comments, no prods. Tony had convinced her that Pamela would tell her in her own time. Meanwhile she hadn't shared her doubts or speculations with anyone, not Linda or Barbara or Jane at bridge, not Cal at the food bank, certainly not anyone at the golf club. What surprised Shirley when she arrived at Pamela's house was the sight of the large motorcycle in the driveway. Shirley walked over to it and examined the machine. The last item on her unusual bucket list was to take a ride on a motorcycle. Was this why Pamela had called her?

"Why Shirley Anne! What's happened to your red hair?"

At the sound of a man's voice Shirley looked up. Who knew

about her resemblance to Anne of Green Gables? The voice was familiar but the old man walking out of her daughter's house was unfamiliar. Who was this stranger who called her Shirley Anne? There was only one man in her life who ever did that. Could it be? Surely not! How could it be Monty? Maybe Pamela had found her father. Shirley had suspected for a long time that her daughter was seeking out the identity of her birth father. On some level, Shirley wanted Pamela to know him, but she could never admit that to herself or to Tony. Now that the secret was revealed it left her stunned. She felt like she'd been left in the dark about intimate family matters. All year she'd been pursuing an impractical list of adventures when what really mattered was the life of her family. Her past had caught up with her.

Now he was standing beside her. "Want to go for a ride?"

"I've never been for a ride on a motorcycle. Is this yours?" Shirley felt mesmerized by his physical presence, by the unexpected, by the motorcycle. It was big and shiny.

"It sure is. Been a long time."

"Where have you been? How did you get here?" Shirley looked at the red motorcycle. The answer was obvious. "What's happened?"

Monty laughed. "To quote Mark Twain, 'I am an old man and have known a great many troubles, but none of them never happened.' I've been in the States, Shirley. I've been there a long time but I heard from Charlie."

"My uncle?" Shirley couldn't keep her head clear. Why was he offering to take her for a ride? Would they disappear together? Would she abandon everyone? The truth was she'd been the one who'd abandoned him.

"The one and only. Want to take a spin?"

"Yes," Shirley simply said as she got on the seat and held

him tight around the waist. As soon as he started the engine it thrummed and she could feel the vibration through her buttocks. The roar of the engine sounded loud when he opened the throttle and drove down the street. She held on for dear life with the wind blowing through her grey hair. Monty drove the motorcycle out of town and headed for the two lane highway that went north. Shirley opened her mouth and laughed. Finally she was taking a ride on a motorcycle, her bucket list complete. This was the life. "Faster," she called.

Monty obliged and gunned the motor. As they came to the long curve that redirected the highway from its straight course around the bay of the shoreline and started heading north west when the wheels underneath them skidded. The last thing Shirley saw was Monty falling over on top of her.

Constable Barry Nickel was the first on the scene. He'd been outside the police station when he'd heard the roar of a motorcycle leaving town. Immediately after the roar came the mournful sound of the train whistle. It was the longest train of the day and the longest whistle among the dozens that announced themselves at the road crossing just outside town nearby. When the accompanying roar of the motorcycle engine suddenly stopped he went to investigate. Now he left the patrol car at an angle across the two lane highway with its red light blinking. Immediately he assessed the situation as a fatality so he called it in thinking it was too early in the morning for such a serious accident. The motorcycle driver must have been going too fast and there were the skid marks to prove him right. Knowing it would take hours for forensics to study the scene he got the yellow tape and blocked the road to any oncoming traffic. Then he radioed again and told his fellow police officers to stop traffic at the crossroads to the north and south of the accident scene.

In the distance he heard the wail of multiple sirens bringing more patrol cars, fire trucks and ambulances to the spot. Now he moved closer to the two dead bodies, one man and one woman. "Oh, my God," he said aloud. On the ground lay Shirley Palmer. He didn't recognize the fellow. How did she get involved in this? In his initial assessment he wrote on his pad that the identified victim seemed to have hit her head on a rock at the side of the highway after being thrown from the motorcycle.

Barry turned toward the arriving vehicles thinking it was going to be a long day.

Chapter 33

Mourning

"I only just met my real father and now he's dead," Pamela wailed into the phone. "And my mother. Please Clinton. She can't be gone."

On the other end of the line Clinton told her he would come straight home.

The phone started emitting a loud dial tone. Pamela was so dazed the female officer who had arrived at her door to tell her that her mother had died in a motorcycle accident took the phone from her hand.

When the female officer had first arrived Pamela instantly identified the male who was killed alongside her mother. At least, she was the one who said the name of the unknown man. Now the female officer led Pamela into the living room and guided her to sit on the couch but Pamela insisted on remaining standing. The shock of what she'd just learned became a dull ache and she started to feel a wave of nausea that she swallowed to keep down. If she sat she would puke. She shook her head no when asked if she would like a glass of water but said, "You go ahead. Pour yourself a glass of water. There's the kitchen."

"No, that's fine, Mrs. Croft. I'll stay with you until your husband gets home."

Pamela didn't know what to do. She waited with the officer who remained standing by her side. Finally the front door opened and Clinton burst in with a determined look on his face like he was going to help in some way that could change everything. He rushed over to his wife and wrapped his arms around her. Then Pamela released a flood of tears. Clinton held her as she sobbed into his shoulder. "What happened?" he asked the female officer.

She explained that there had been a motorcycle accident on Highway #2 and his mother-in-law, Shirley Palmer, and a man whom Pamela thought must be Monty Caragiale, were found dead at the scene of the accident.

Clinton nodded as if he understood but his face showed utter confusion.

"I'll leave you now but will return later to have you come down to the morgue to identify the bodies, if that's alright?"

"What about my father-in-law? Does he know?"

"Yes, I understand Chief Schroeder went to his house."

"Yeah, that was nice of him. Tony knows the Chief." Clinton put the palm of his hand over his wife's head and felt her scalp beneath her hair. His mind raced with thoughts of actions he would have to take: go to the high school and get Tim, phone the university and tell Lily, call work to tell them he wouldn't be returning today. Then he thought that Pamela probably needed to alert clients or appointments, but first he had to sort out his confusion. She had been so excited over the weekend when Charlie phoned to say he had been in contact with Monty and told him where she lived. She had wanted to keep it a secret from the children and her mother until she'd heard from Monty. She kept calling him her 'birth father'. Clinton pulled himself away and looked down at his sobbing wife. "Do you want to tell me what happened?"

Pamela lifted her head and nodded yes. Her eyes were bloodshot from crying. The ends of her hair were wet from her tears. Her breathing was laboured from her sobbing. She sat on the couch and Clinton sat beside her. "He arrived this morning soon after you'd left for work and Tim had gone to school."

"Monty?"

"Yes. He just appeared out of nowhere on our doorstep. He was so gregarious I was bowled over by him. He was full of boisterous greetings as if we had known each other all along and he'd just been away awhile and now he'd returned and he was so glad to see me. He said I looked a lot like his mother. That I even had her small feet. Isn't that silly? He noticed my feet."

"Yes," Clinton said. "You do have small feet. You always say that when buying shoes because you can always find a pair on sale."

Pamela sat in silence for a time before continuing. "He told me about his family in the States and how he'd been a draft dodger but then was able to return home. He took care of his mother and never married again or had any children. He'd been so hurt by what'd happened. He'd heard from his buddies that Shirley was doing well and he didn't want to spoil things for her. So I asked him if he wanted to see her now that he was here and he said he did so I called Mom and convinced her to come over. It's all my fault!"

Pamela grew hysterical. Clinton hated these moments when she was out of control. He never knew how to calm her. He certainly couldn't use humour in this circumstance. "It's not your fault. They're both adults and they did what they chose to do."

"But if I hadn't been so determined to meet him this wouldn't have happened."

"But you didn't send them off on a motorcycle ride. Did he arrive on a motorcycle?"

"Yes he did but I didn't know that at first." Pamela gasped for air. "I didn't see what he was driving. After calling Mom he watched for her from the window. The whole time he was waiting he talked about himself. How his mother had died in the summer. How he was going to go up north to visit Charlie. He said when he died he wanted his ashes spread at the lodge." Pamela choked.

"There, there," Clinton said rubbing her back.

"I just don't understand. Why was he telling me all those things? Did he know he was going to die? Did he have a premonition?"

"I doubt it, honey. He was probably feeling comfortable with you. You were his closest family even though he'd only just met you."

Pamela inhaled deeply. "When Mom arrived he went outside to greet her and that's when I saw them standing beside the motorcycle and the next thing I knew they were gone."

"Shirley always wanted to take a ride on a motorcycle."

"She did?" Pamela looked up at him with wide eyes.

"It was one of the items on her bucket list. Like holding a demonstration."

"And going to the prom."

"And being in the prom parade."

"And smoking pot."

"Shirley missed out on a lot."

Pamela sank into the couch and let her head flop against the back cushion. "I just can't believe it. It's so horrible. It doesn't seem real."

"You're in shock. What about Tim? I think I should phone the high school and go get him."

Rolling her head sideways Pamela stared at him and agreed he should.

Tony arrived home to a heap of sheets piled on the floor. It was a strange sight but stranger still was the call he'd received from Albert Schroeder asking to meet him at the house. The man had tracked him down at the seniors' residence where Tony had gone early in the morning in response to a distressed call from his mother. She'd lost the t.v. remote control flicker. Tony found it under her night stand. Apparently none of the staff could locate it for her. Neither could they change the channels without it. Tony was still puffed and slightly out of breath from having gotten down on his hands and knees to retrieve it. His mother seemed to know where it was and had told the staff where it could possibly be but none of them had crawled around on the floor to fetch it. Maud liked to watch the breakfast show before eating breakfast so he'd left her content. Tony was pleased to have started his day by making someone happy. He wondered where Shirley had gotten to?

Not surprised by the knock on the door Tony opened it to greet Albert and invited him inside. Being too polite to question why Albert was visiting him early in the morning he remained silent until the chief spoke. "I'm sorry, Tony, I have some deeply disturbing news. It's about Shirley."

"Shirley?"

"Yes. There's no other way for me to say it. She died in an accident on Highway #2."

"Why was she there? I don't remember her saying she was going out this morning. Are you sure it was her?"

"Yes. Constable Barry Nickel identified her."

"The one she struck?"

"Yes."

Tony started to shake. "Good God. What kind of an accident? Was anyone else hurt?"

"Yes, the driver of the motorcycle."

"She crashed into a motorcycle?"

"She was riding on the motorcycle."

"Good God. Why was she on a motorcycle?" Tony could feel tears welling up behind his eyes.

"Pamela explained the circumstances to one of our officers."

"Pamela?"

"Her husband is with her now."

"Oh, I see."

"Would you like to call her?"

"Yes, yes," Tony said rising nervously.

"Do you want me to wait with you while you phone her?"

"No, that won't be necessary." He started to walk away but stopped and turned. "Thank you Albert. Do I have to identify her or anything like that?"

"No, that won't be necessary. Pamela has agreed to do that."

"I don't want her to do it. That's going to be very hard on her."

"Since she can identify both bodies it's for the best."

"She can? I see." Although he didn't see. He really didn't understand.

When Albert left Tony stood behind the closed door and wept. He hadn't cried real tears since his father passed away and he did that in private too. He placed his palms on the door to steady himself trying to understand that Shirley was gone. She was very much alive when he'd left her that morning. He ached.

He leaned his forehead on the door and felt the ache throughout his entire body. He wept until his nose bubbled. He kept crying as his tears ran down his cheeks. He put his hands over his face and sobbed. "Please, dear Lord. Don't do this."

It was many minutes until Tony composed himself enough to dial Pamela. What he heard truly stunned him.

Chapter 34

Visitation

On Friday evening the immediate family gathered at the funeral home, at least five of them did, not six. They had picked out an open casket for Shirley. It was a decision made based on the good appearance of her face. The only injury she'd suffered was on the back of her head where she'd hit the rock. Holding hands they stood alongside the casket and shared a quiet time together staring down at wife, mother, grandmother. Then they broke apart and formed a line to greet those who came to pay their respects.

First through the door was a thin man with a pale face. "Hi Cal," Tim said taking a step forward. He introduced the man to his grandfather who robustly shook his hand. "So glad you came and I got to meet you," Tony said. "Shirley always spoke highly of you and the work you're doing at the food bank."

"I want to thank you for your generous donation. It's made a huge difference for us. I'm going to miss that gal. She was a real trooper."

Tony blinked back the tears welling up in his eyes. Knowing that his wife was loved by others made him suddenly long for her and their good times together. He proudly watched his grandson.

Tim escorted Cal down the line and introduced him to his mother and father. Then he and Lily stood beside him as he watched the video that Tim had prepared from photographs. When Cal said he must have a real talent Tim admitted it was easy to do using the machine at the supermarket.

"She had quite a life, didn't she?"

Pamela gently called her children back to meet Albert Schroeder and his wife Hilda. "I'm so sorry for your loss," Hilda said. "She must have been lots of fun."

"She was," Tim said.

"The last thing I heard her say was 'Have a safe journey' when we went to the golf club to have dinner before I left for university," Lily said and then started to cry.

"I'm sure you'll keep having lots of wonderful memories of her."

"Thanks," Lily said to Hilda while drying her eyes.

Linda Leach came with her family. She gave Tony a big hug and introduced her grandson, Rupert. "Lily's date for the prom," Tony said extending his hand in welcome. He asked where the lad was studying.

Rupert told him, then added, "I decided to come home this weekend when I heard what had happened to Lily's grandmother. She was really nice to us."

"I'm going to miss her," Linda said and started to sob. Rupert put his arm around her shoulders and guided her down the greeting line. "Hi," he said to Lily.

"Hi," Lily said.

Linda gave Lily a hug and said, "I always had such fun with your grandma."

"I know," Lily said shaking her head to hold back her tears.

"We did too."

"Oh look at that," Linda said turning to look at the pictures that were moving across the screen. "There we are on the cruise when Clarence was alive." She stood in front of the screen mesmerized by the display of the trip that took them around the world.

"Hello Michael," Tony said to the principal.

"Hello Mr. Wilson," Tim said.

"What a tragedy," Michael Wilson said. "I'm sorry she went before her time."

"Thank you for coming," Pamela said.

"You take as much time as you need," he said to his student.

"I think I'll be back on Monday, Tuesday latest," Tim said.

Len introduced his wife Brandy. "I was her hairdresser," she said to Tony.

"It's very nice of you to come, both of you. You've been a great help over these past few weeks," Tony said.

"Always happy to help out," Len said.

By now the line was backing up. Tony thrust his arm out to shake Max's hand. "Thank you for coming. You too, Nadia."

"We were so shocked to hear what happened. She'll be missed." Nadia walked down the line and gave their condolences to Clinton. They stood talking to him for a few minutes.

"I'm Eva Wilhelm," a woman said to Tony. "And my husband, Jack. We have a farm close to town. I went to school with Shirley. We weren't close but I got to know her more lately when she came to shop at the Farmers' Market."

"Yes," Tony said greeting the couple. "Shirley liked going there."

Jack nodded to Tony and mumbled that he was sorry for his loss.

Ramsey Reisch thrust his hand out to Tony. Then he clasped

him on his upper arm. "Rose and I will be there tomorrow. You need help you just call. Anytime. Understand?"

"Thanks, Ramsey. You've both already been a great help. I don't know how I would have gotten through the week without you."

"Well, you just remember what I said because there will come a time next week when you're all alone with everyone gone back to their normal routines and life won't be the same for you. You know where we are."

"That's very kind of you."

Ramsey went down the line giving his condolences to each and every member of the family before being accosted by Linda Leach who said he had to see the pictures that Tim had included of the cruise that they took together. Ramsey stood beside Linda spellbound by the show. He laughed. "We sure did fill our bucket list," he said giving Linda a quick hug.

By now the funeral parlor was crowded. Noise came from the hallway where people were waiting to enter. It seemed like the whole town had come out to share their condolences with a family who had suffered a sudden loss. Inside the room voices rose under the display where well wishers had stopped to talk to one another after looking at the photographs and mementos. It seemed Shirley's whole life was put on view. After two hours of receiving friends the family was left alone. Tim and Clinton gathered up the video and photographs. Pamela and Lily took the mementos. Tony stayed behind to talk to the funeral director about plans for tomorrow. Once everything was confirmed he left with the guest book under his arm. It had many pages of signed signatures. He was surprised at the outpouring of sympathy. His initial shock had given way over the week to profound grieving. On many days he had comforted Pamela who had gone from self-blame to feelings of shame to deep mourning for her mother. There'd been an endless list of arrangements to make. He'd supported Pamela in having Monty cremated. They had his ashes put in an urn for Charlie to take back with him. He'd arrived earlier in the day with Johnny who wanted to stay with his grandmother through the evening. Neither he nor Charlie liked the idea of seeing people in town for the first time in years on such an occasion. Johnny thought it would detract from the real purpose of the visitation at the funeral home. Tony did not argue with his son since he would be present at the funeral as a pallbearer. That was clearly enough exposure.

Driving home alone in his car Tony thought about what Ramsey Reisch had said about the upcoming week. As well as losing his wife on Monday Tony and all investors like him had been dealing with a market crash. Everything was in decline. He would need Ramsey's advice on what to do. So far he'd done nothing because he was dealing with profound grief, his own and his family's, but that may have been a good thing. Maybe it was best to just hold on until everything settled down again. Ramsey and Rose were good friends. The two couples had been through many troubles together. Tony knew he could count on their support without being stabbed in the back.

It was Rose who'd helped him with writing the obituary for the local newspaper:

Shirley Palmer died suddenly on Monday, September 15, 2008, at the age of 60. Beloved wife of Anthony Palmer, dear mother of Pamela (Clinton) and Johnny, loving Grandma of Lily and Tim. She will be sorely missed by family and friends, especially Jane Palmer, Barbara Bletch, and Linda Leach. Visitation at Dellport Funeral Home on Friday night between 7 and 9 pm. Service at St. Anthony Church on Saturday at 11 am. followed by a Reception at Dellport Golf and Country Club. In lieu of flowers donations to the Food Bank appreciated.

Chapter 35

The Funeral

The church sat on the site of the original place of worship built by the first settlers to the community. In honor of their predecessors this church had a stained glass window made of Saint Anthony, the patron saint of farm animals. It pictured him in the middle of the pane dressed in brown raiments. He was practically life-size, an iconic figure who was a Coptic saint from Egypt and father of all saints who went into the wilderness. The top section of the pane showed Saint Anthony facing these other saints who wanted his blessing. Opposite on top was a cave where he'd lived like a hermit. The bottom quadrant pictured farm animals, some sheep and a donkey. The ever-tempting devil was behind him, his red horns the most colourful pieces of stained glass in the entire window.

Anthony Palmer was always told that he'd been named after this saint even though his family weren't farmers but merchants. His father, Elmo Palmer, had instilled in him respect for all of God's creatures. Now he thought about his father and how Shirley would join him in heaven. He'd never told his father about his crisis of faith. Now Tony was reminded of that time when in church with his family he thought how it was all bogus. How could a reasonable person believe such stories? He was home after finishing a business degree in university and feeling very urban and cosmopolitan. At the time his doubting thoughts filled him with grief. How could he tell his family about his disbelief when they'd been so supportive and trusting? It was at that time Shirley had returned to town with Pamela in tow. When Tony had first met them he'd immediately thought he could rehabilitate himself by caring for them. Rather than suffer from a lack of purpose, he could restore some measure to his life.

Now with her gone he refused to accept that everything had come undone. Anthony Palmer walked along the side aisle of the church and stopped in front of this large stained glass window where he felt under its protection. There he stood patiently waiting for the family to assemble at the front of the church. He saw Tim walk quickly along the aisle looking for him. Both were fighting their tears. Tony spoke to his grandson admitting that they were clearly moved by such a profound loss. Yet Tim answered by complaining that he'd overheard some people saying his grandmother was running away with Monty when they crashed and they got what they deserved.

Tony felt he would burst with indignation and he clutched Tim to him as more tears flowed. "Never mind them," Tony said, patting the youth's back. "They don't know what they're saying. People like gossip more than truth." He drew away and encouraged Tim to walk bravely back to join the others. As they strode down the aisle he greeted those who sat in the pews waiting for the funeral service to begin.

One of the helpers at the back of the church was a young man. Tony introduced him to Tim, "Matthew, the Reverend's son. I'm pleased you've made yourself available, Matthew."

Tim shook Matthew's hand saying he was pleased to meet him and that he hadn't seen him around town.

"I go to a seminary school out of town."

"So you have a biblical name?" Tim asked.

"Yes, you could say that, but then, so do you."

Tim smiled. "We've never gone to church."

"So you've never been baptized?"

When Tim said he hadn't Matthew said he could teach him the scriptures if he would like to be more familiar with the teachings. "I don't know Timothy as well as Matthew which I have memorized."

"Really? Quote chapter 7," Tim said challenging the young man as he would a boy in the playground.

"Judge not, that ye be not judged. For with what judgment ye judge, ye shall be judged: and with what measure ye mete, it shall be measured to you again."

"That's so relevant," Tim said.

Matthew bowed his head.

Outside Tony saw that Johnny was helping Maud up the front steps. She held the railing leaning on her right hand and he held her left forearm. When they reached the top an usher took her into the church. Another usher directed Johnny and Tim to sit where the pallbearers should sit.

Ushers handed out the order of service to people as they arrived. Since Shirley and Tony had not gotten around to discussing their personal wishes Tony had to make all the decisions about how to celebrate his wife's life. Reverend Brathwaite was very helpful. On the front was a coloured picture of Shirley taken recently on the golf course. He liked the photo because it was taken outside and Shirley liked being outside. He always attributed that preference in her to why she hated housework so much. Above the picture were the dates of her birth and death: October 14, 1947 – September 15, 2008. They'd had a big celebration last year when she'd turned 60. They'd made plans to go away in October, somewhere close like the new resort a few towns away that had a golf course with good food.

Tony took his seat in the front pew beside his mother. Pamela sat beside them with Lily. Clinton sat with the pallbearers. When the organ began Tony stared at the closed casket that was adorned with a bouquet of yellow roses. They stood to sing the hymn 'All Things Bright And Beautiful' which was one of Shirley's favourites. They sat while Rev. Brathwaite led them in prayer. Tony began the Family Remembrances and Reflections by reading from St. Luke. Verses 22, 23, 24, and 25 that were printed for everyone to follow: "All things are delivered to me," Tony began, " of my Father: and no man knoweth who the Son is, but the Father; and who the Father is, but the Son, and he to whom the Son will reveal him. And he turned him unto his disciples, and said privately, Blessed are the eyes which see the things that ye see; For I tell you, and many prophets and kings have desired to see those things which ye see, and have not seen them; and to hear those things which ye hear, and have not heard them. And, behold, a certain lawyer stood up, and tempted him, saying, Master, what shall I do to inherit eternal life?"

He sat down and Tim walked to the front. He spoke without notes. "My Grandmother, Shirley Anne Montgomery Caragiale Palmer, was the one who taught me to make promises by saying, 'Cross my heart and hope to die.' When I did make her a promise or swear that what I was saying was the truth, the whole truth, and nothing but the truth, she would say, 'See you in heaven'. So Grandma, see you in heaven."

Tony heard Lily sob and he turned to her. When he was making arrangements for the funeral service she'd said she was too emotional to speak in front of everyone and he'd comforted her by saying that not everyone could display their emotions in public without choking up. That was why he chose to read the written word. Pamela took hold of Lily's hand. Tony turned back to face the front and continued listening to his grandson's heartwarming eulogy. Tim was a very brave hearted young man. Sometimes it took grief to make a person mature and Tim was maturing at a very young age.

Next up came Charlie Long. "It's been a long time since I've seen some of you and I'm sorry it's on an occasion like this that we meet again. I'm even sorrier that I haven't seen my sister's daughter in decades. It's been too long, though I am grateful to have met her wonderful family, Pamela and her husband Clinton, their two children, Tim and Lily. I look forward to getting to know them better. I've been very happy recently to have my great nephew helping me, Shirley's and Tony's son, Johnny. What's more important than family? I never had none of my own and I'm grateful that Shirley's family have welcomed me with open arms. She made everyone's lives better. What more good can you do on this earth than that? May you rest in peace, Shirley. We will never forget you."

Linda Leach was the last to brave the public eye. She spoke through tears, saying a person could never have had a better friend than Shirley Palmer and she was going to miss her every day.

After singing another hymn Rev. Brathwaite read from Proverbs. The words were printed in the order of service: "That I might make thee know the certainty of the words of truth; that thou mightest answer the words of truth to them that send unto Thee? Rob not the poor, because he is poor: neither oppress the afflicted in the gate: For the Lord will plead their cause, and spoil the soul of those that spoiled them."

At the end of the service the pallbearers: Johnny Palmer, Tim and Clinton Croft, Charles Long, Ramsey Reisch and Cal Ford, carried the casket down the aisle of the church and outside to the waiting hearse. First the family followed then the other mourners. They got into their vehicles and lined up behind the hearse that carried Shirley's casket. A police motorcade led them to the cemetery. Those who didn't go to the Committal Service at the graveside headed directly to Dellport Golf and Country Club for the reception.

Chapter 36

Reception

A celebration of life involves stories. As soon as Johnny arrived he was accosted by a few men whom he'd known as a teenager. Their talk quickly turned to reminiscing about old times. They crowded around the end of the table where a stack of sandwiches quickly disappeared. Most of the talk was about boats: size, speed, make.

Pamela found Felicia. They hugged and wept. "Sorry, so sorry," Felicia said through her tears, "I didn't come earlier. So sad I didn't see her again."

"I know," Pamela said, "but I'm glad to see you here and that you came all this way. I've missed you." She clung to Felicia, her second mother, her ersatz sister.

"Paolo put the house up for sale. I'm helping clear everything out. We're moving out west."

"Yes, I heard. That's nice for you. You'll be near your son."

"And the rest of my family. But you're my family too," Felicia said. "Just not my blood family. But you will always feel like family to me. I'm so sorry I didn't say goodbye last time. I was so scared."

Pamela pulled her head back to look more closely at Felicia. "What do you mean, scared?"

"About the police and jail. It makes me nervous."

"Oh, I see," Pamela said realizing that she knew what Felicia was saying because of her background and past, but that she didn't fully comprehend her fear. What must this woman think of them? She'd been through so much in her early years and had remained so dutiful during her time with them. "You must keep in touch. I don't want to lose you again."

"No. I will not abandon you. Never again."

"Silly, you didn't abandon me. You did what you had to do to take care of yourself."

"I'm so happy to see Johnny back here with his family. Who is Charlie?"

"Charlie is Shirley's uncle. Her mother's brother."

"She never speak of him."

"No, but we visited him at his lodge this summer." Pamela started to weep. "He helped me find my dad."

"Monty? The one who was killed?"

Pamela nodded.

"So he knew your uncle?"

"Yes. That's where I was born. In northern Ontario. But now I've lost my mother and my father."

"No, you have Tony. He's your real father. He raised you. He take good care of you."

Pamela nodded. How to explain? What was there to explain? Did it need explaining?

"Paolo said Shirley got into more trouble after I left?"

Pamela laughed. "My mother never stopped. She got Tim into trouble too. She had to do community service at the food bank as punishment."

"At least no one end up in jail."

Pamela drew Felicia close and again hugged her.

Lily and Rupert stood awkwardly together and asked each

other questions about their respective universities. Then Rupert said, "Your grandmother really was fun, wasn't she? We had the best prom and parade. When I talk to the other students at university I know ours was better. Some of them got too drunk to remember what it was like."

"Our parents' association lobbied for a dry prom."

"You don't need to drink to have fun."

"No, but it is part of our culture. Just look who's here and what they're doing," Lily said angling her head in the direction of the bar.

Rupert turned around to look. "Including my grandmother. She's really broken up about Shirley. They were good friends going way back."

"Yes, we'll stay friends, won't we Rupert?"

Rupert smiled at her. "Of course we will. Even when we graduate and get married."

Lily laughed.

Tony stepped away from the bar and took a good look around the room. Everyone stood in groups talking, eating, and drinking. Johnny was with his old high school buddies and distant cousins. Pamela was hugging Felicia. Lily was laughing with Rupert. He thought 'Life is for the living'. He was going to miss his wife but he had all of this. Was it enough? He hoped he could find comfort in what he had. He expected to feel lonely and alone despite his blessings.

He choked and turned away not wanting the crowd see his tears. There in the far corner of the room near the orangery Jane sat with Maud. They seemed alone but they weren't missing out on growing old together. Tony prayed he would live to a ripe old age like his mother.

Book Club Questions
and
Discussion Points

Novel Structure

– As a reader do you see a redemptive arc in this manuscript?

– Some might consider this to be a picaresque novel. Do you agree?

– Do you see character development in the main character, Shirley and in what way?

– If so what changes do you see, if not why?

– Do you see this novel structure as being more stasis or transformational.

– Do we as readers ask the main character to teach us something?

– Did this novel provoke conversation and discussion?

Meaning of Life

– Do you agree that Shirley reads no deeper into the meaning of life than what fate has dealt her?

– She loves life and accepts her attitude as a given. Is it that she feels entitled – if so How?

– Does she simply think everyone can and will without question find happiness. Is she unusual?

– Shirley had a bucket list of what she felt she had missed out on. That list structures the narrative of the novel but does it serve to satisfy her in the end?

– In the end does she miss out on life? How does her bucket list compare to yours.

– In what ways do you see that love is an important theme in this novel?

– There are many kinds of love: maternal, brotherly, free, parental, romantic. How many kinds of love did Shirley find?

– In what ways is the pull of family an important theme to Shirley and in the book in general?

– Instincts drive people to huddle around the strong. In what ways do family ties keep Shirley's family loyal to her?

– In what ways do you perceive the town of Dellport as a character in the novel?

– What other characters in the novel do you find interesting?

What Readers Should **NOT** Miss
from
What Shirley Missed

"A celebration of life involves stories." This is the first line of the book's last Chapter. This is what Donna Wootton's book is about. Family issues, secrets and stories are inevitable and ideal for authors to explore. These are delicate themes, but worth writing about as Wootton does very well. Everyone has a family, everyone weaves through the "slings and arrows" of family conflicts. *What Shirley Missed* gives us a taste of what we know only so well, what many of us have experienced. The author does it in a fast-moving, snow-balling way, unfolding events from the very beginning.

The characters are wonderfully credible. Wootton paints a picture of their behavior with a confident hand. She exploits their predicaments letting mini-plots in the conversations rise and shock the reader. These fuel the crescendo of the main plot when Pamela, Shirley's daughter, bursts into the room: *"How could you?"* Pamela barged past her mother. *"What were you thinking?" she said as she stomped into the hallway without hugging her mother."* Once the conversation starts, it is one discovery after another. Wootton is skilled at providing surprise turns that create suspense and interest.

To my delight, I detected nuances of humor as well, despite the tense situations, in Shirley´s thoughts trailing off to her many preoccupations wondering what she had done that upset her daughter and the family, then to her comments about her pregnancy. Such feeling remained with me throughout the book. On page sixteen I was already determined to go all the way to the end of this fine story.

Another example of the author's skill as a writer is her time interplay with scenes, the overlapping of events that shift from the family conversation to Shirley´s thoughts, both to the far past and to the moment her husband and daughter are pressing her to talk. The author succeeds in charging the atmosphere with more and more questions, which gives Chapter 1 material enough to fill the next 200 pages.

What follows turns into an excellent meditation about immigration, doubt, faith, human values, vanity, old age and much more. As if this is not enough, she covers the philosophical ideas of how life unfurls, people´s lives, dreams and sacrifices, and of course finally, death. This confers Wootton´s style, a plasticity that I enjoyed as a reader. There are social-psychological ramifications at play throughout the book. Wootton handles them chapter by chapter, through the characters´ reflections and aspirations.

The author moves on different themes, touches upon them or develops them, but they all pivot around the main plot: the human sketches and circumstances described by Wootton are understandable and believable, a quality I appreciate as a reader.

The story, the plot, the characters and the message are valid for, those like me, who have accumulated anecdotes and memories with the years. It is helpful too for younger generations experiencing life. *What Shirley Missed* is a welcome voyage into people like us, no overdoing in its proposal, no superfluous lines and no unnecessary characters.

Wootton writes with ease and insight, showing ins and outs, ups and downs in the scenes, the inner lacking and desires bubbling in Shirley, which affect those around her. Wootton also unveils society´s multi-cultural fabric and traditions. Objectivity, elegance and poise flow from her seasoned pen, and looks at the gentle threads of intergenerational family interaction.

I did notice the fineness with which Wootton outlines the different people´s hopes and subjects of conversation. Solidly based on family values and synergy, the author paints, beyond words, the cultural input brought in by a diverse inflow of immigrants, exceptionally harmonized alongside the existing one. Family is the core, the forge and springboard that Wootton uses to venture into the world seeking warmth and love.

Wootton also does well, displaying for the reader, a variety of events, customs, and musts in social attachments. She knits the chapters together not only on a temporal plane of space, place and concrete names, but also blends with the ethereal construct of time.

I was pleased by the author´s dedication to the prom. In Cuba, one important date in the life of a teenage girl is the "quince party." In Cuban culture this party is held for a girl when she turns fifteen. It is a celebratory day with joyful rituals and ceremonies. It includes a convertible car parade for the birthday girl, photo sessions, new clothes, party with friends, etc. The author's intention to give the reader all the details of the prom struck home for me.

The prom, the bridge game, the market, the beach, home, the golf tournament, the demonstration, the police station, the funerals, etc. are the author's socially-projected "alibi" to ripen the novel's plot. They are the contexts where human thoughts are ignited and acts performed and made visible by Wootton.

Enjoy this new book by Donna Wootton. Readers should not miss it, as they should not miss the author's graceful depiction of people and places, of circumstances and fate. *What Shirley Missed* celebrates living and in doing so has left us a story that deserves to be read and pondered.

M.Sc. Miguel Ángel Olivé Iglesias
Associate Professor, University of Holguín, Cuba
CCLA Cuban President & The Ambassador Editor-in-chief

A Short Bio Note:

Donna Wootton is an author and retired teacher who lives in Port Hope, ON, Canada. Her most recent work is an ebook titled *Isadora & Lucia*. Her short stories, poems, and nonfiction have appeared in four anthologies: most recently, *Hill Spirits III*, published in 2017. The first *Hill Spirits* anthology and *Grandmother and Me* were both published in 2012. Her book published in Dec., 2009, is a creative nonfiction account of her father who was a charter inductee into the Canadian Lacrosse Hall of Fame. It is called *MOON REMEMBERED The Life of Lacrosse Goalie Lloyd 'Moon' Wootton* and is published by Ginger Press in Owen Sound where her father was born and raised. As well, she has a novel, *Leaving Paradise*, that is available at local independent bookstores and libraries. Her haiku poetry has been published in Japan with the Asahi Network.